Forgiveness is God's command.

—Martin Luther

Savannah Secrets

Season's Meetings

ANNE MARIE RODGERS

Guideposts

Danbury, Connecticut

Season's Meetings

The Interview, Part 1

Mason Denton
Grade 6
Effingham County Middle School
English Language Arts

My assignment: Interview a senior citizen with an interesting life story and write a transcript of the interview. (Transcript = a written or printed record of material originally presented in another way, such as an interview.)

Interview with my great-grandfather Sumner Denton, age 93, Guyton, GA, 10/12/2020.

Interviewer: *Great-granddaddy, you showed me an old newspaper photo of you and your sisters and brother from when you were little. What did the newspaper say?*

SD: It said, "Five Children for Sale. Five children in rural Guyton, Georgia, will be sold or given away by their widowed mother, who can no longer care for them." A man from the newspaper came and took the picture. I had the newspaper for a long time, and I pestered the lady I worked for until she told me what it said. After I learned to read, I memorized it. Two little sentences. You wouldn't think two little sentences could say so much about somebody's life. Sometimes I looked at it, trying to fix everything I could in my mind about the others—my little sisters and brother.

Interviewer: How did you feel about getting sold?

SD: Well, I didn't really understand what was happening until after, when I was taken away, and it was years before I found out Mrs. Healy had paid money for me. But being taken away was pretty terrible. How could anybody sell their children? I remember the day my first child was born. I looked down at her little red, squished face and wondered how anyone could give their own child away. I know it's not my place to judge. Still, I wish, just once, I could go back in time and talk to my mama, ask her if it really was so bad that she had to sell us. Like we were furniture or something. But then, I guess it was, since she died little more'n a year later. Mrs. Healy, the lady I worked for, she said Mama was hysterical and she drowned. Mama didn't even know how to swim, and she would never have gone in the pond. I couldn't figure how she could have drowned. It wasn't until a lot of years had passed that I understood Mama had probably killed herself. I imagine she was pretty sad over my father's death and the fact that she couldn't provide for the five of us. That's probably what led to her selling us. And selling us off is probably what led her to kill herself. At least, that's how I see it. Makes it a little easier to forgive her, you know? She must have been one heartsick lady.

Interviewer: *Great-granddaddy, what do you remember about taking the picture?*

SD: The newspaper photo? I remember the day it was taken, probably because that day was so different from every other day. First, Ma bathed all five of us, from me right down to the baby. Then she dressed us all in the least-worn-out of our clothes. No shoes, because who had money for shoes during the Depression? She made us sit on the front porch so we wouldn't get dirty, and she gave me a piece of candy to break into five tiny little pieces so every kid could have one. I was in charge of making sure little Tillie didn't choke. She was barely a year old, and I was seven. What kind of job was that for a seven-year-old? Mama was crying in the kitchen when the man came. I say kitchen, but we only had the two rooms. It wasn't much, but after Daddy died, we had to move outta the place where we were before. That little shack was where Tillie was born, without a single grown-up female around to help. Just me'n Bobbie Dee and the two little ones. Anyway, we looked at the man, and I called Mama, but none of us moved, because Ma said she'd tan our hides if we got dirty. So, the man set up this contraption on long sticks and set his black picture box on top of it. We didn't know at the time it was a camera and a tripod, but I'll never forget it. He wanted Mama in the picture too, but she wouldn't. I don't remember the For Sale sign at all, but I couldn't read back then, because I never went to school till I was at Mrs. Healy's.

Interviewer: *Who was Mrs. Healy?*

SD: Mrs. Healy, she was a widow. She's the one who bought me. I went first. I didn't want to go, but she handed two dollars to Mama and told me, "Come on, boy," so I went. Didn't want the little kids to see me cry or carry on. Mama wouldn't even say goodbye or hug me or nothin'. She just put her apron over her head and ran inside. I understand that now, but down deep inside where that little kid lives, it still makes me hurt. I never saw my mama again. First thing Mrs. Healy asked was could I read. And when I told her I never went to school, she like to had a fit. She made me go to school every day, and as it turned out, I was good at school, at reading and spelling and figuring. Mrs. Healy made me go to church every Sunday with her too. I didn't love church like I loved school, but church made me a better person. Church helped me forgive my mother. My daddy too, for up and dying and leaving us to starve and get sold. Church helped me learn to look at the good things in any situation. I've been in a few tight spots in my life, and I always remember to thank Mrs. Healy. That old woman was my guardian angel right here on earth, and I was sorry when she died.

Chapter One

"Thanks for going with me, Meredith. This was as wonderful as I remember!" Julia Foley smiled at her dear friend and business partner, Meredith Bellefontaine, as they descended one side of the steps that flanked the graceful marble-columned porch of Devender-Chisholm House. They had just toured the main floor of the Regency-style mansion and enjoyed the stunning holiday theme with which the Chisholm family had decorated their home. Every December, the Downtown Neighborhood Association in Savannah held a holiday tour of homes and inns in the city's National Historic Landmark District. This year, they'd chosen the first Saturday in December for the occasion.

"The whole tour was enjoyable, but the Chisholm home has never been on the tour before that I can remember," Meredith mused. "I've never been inside. It's incredible, even without the gorgeous holiday decor."

"Well, hello, girls." A car had pulled to the curb, and a young woman was helping an older lady from the car. There weren't many people in Savannah who could pull off calling Meredith and Julia "girls," but this dowager was one of them.

Julia recognized the elderly woman instantly. "Good afternoon, Miss Cora. We just had the privilege of touring your beautiful home.

It was my absolute favorite this year." She and Meredith came to a halt on the sidewalk.

"Why, thank you, dear." Cora Butler Chisholm had to be well over eighty, but she still carried herself straight as an arrow, and her silvery hair was elegantly styled around her face. She wore white wool slacks with red flats, and a red wool shawl was flung with élan over the upper half of her body. "I had a nice long lunch with my great-granddaughter today," she said, indicating the young woman hovering protectively. "But this is some very good luck. I had intended to give your agency a call this week. Could I convince you to come and chat with me for a few minutes?"

Intrigued, Julia glanced at Meredith, who nodded, her eyes alight with curiosity.

"We'd like nothing better," Julia declared.

"Wonderful!" Miss Cora turned to her great-grandchild. "Camille, thank you for driving. It was delightful to catch up with you. I'll see you at your presentation." She held out her arms.

The young woman carefully hugged her frail elder and kissed each of her cheeks. "It was great to see you too, Great-grandmamma. Love you."

"Camille is one of this year's debutantes being presented by the Cotillion Club," Miss Cora told Julia and Meredith proudly as they watched the black BMW pull away from the curb.

"How lovely," Meredith said. "You must be proud."

"I was a debutante in my youth," Miss Cora told them. "As were my daughters and their daughters. I may be eighty-eight, but I'll never forget my coming-out. Of course, it used to mean much more than it does to these modern young girls."

Julia smiled, although she refrained from speaking. The Christmas Cotillion in Savannah had presented its first debutantes in 1817, making it the oldest debutante ball in the United States. (Although, sadly, with slavery still in full practice at that time, no Black young ladies were allowed to participate in the debutante experience.)

Julia had not been presented in her youth, since her working-class family was not of the caliber to receive such a distinguished invitation. But Meredith, born into one of the city's oldest wealthy families, had been a deb. Julia wasn't sure she loved the idea of young women being presented like delicate flowers in the twenty-first century, but like many Savannah notions that were less than contemporary, a few folks still clung to the two-century-old tradition.

Things were changing though. The path to becoming a debutante was no longer quite as exclusive as it once had been. A few girls from families who had acquired their wealth more recently and whose surnames did not appear in the ranks of the old guard from many decades past had begun to populate the ranks of the debs. And this year, like the last several, there were barely more than a half-dozen young women being presented, a far cry from the large groups of yesteryear.

"Help me up these steps, and we'll have a little something to eat and drink," Miss Cora said.

With Meredith and Julia each lending an arm for support, they mounted the steps and returned to the lovely home, where the tour guides were just gathering their things and preparing to depart. Although many of the homeowners showed their own homes, Miss Cora and her family had chosen not to be present during the tours.

"Julia." A woman with expertly high- and lowlighted blond hair stepped forward, arms outstretched. "How nice to see you. I was with another tour group when you came in."

As she recognized the speaker, Julia allowed her smile to dim just a fraction to something less genuine and more impersonal. "Hello, Gaye." She continued to offer her arm to Miss Cora and ignored the offered embrace. "It looked like it was a busy afternoon."

"We were full from the minute the doors opened." Gaye dropped her arms.

"Miss Cora, have you met Gaye Strieter?" Julia might have skipped the introductions, but good manners prevailed, and the elderly lady was looking quite interested in their conversation.

"I don't believe I have. It's a pleasure, dear," Miss Cora drawled. "Thank you for your part in showing my home today."

"The pleasure was entirely mine," Gaye assured her. She paused, and it looked as if she was going to say something more. But then she adjusted her purse on her shoulder and gave a little wiggle of her fingers. "I must be going. Y'all take care now."

"Take care." Julia joined Meredith and Miss Cora in a brief fare-well before turning away. Of all the people she hadn't expected to see today, Gaye Strieter topped the list. They'd been good friends once, long ago in what felt like a different lifetime, all the way from elementary school through high school. Neither had come from a wealthy family, and money, or lack of it, had never seemed to matter, until they went to different colleges and Gaye decided that to become upwardly mobile, she'd have to ditch Julia.

Miss Cora flung her brilliant shawl over a chair and beckoned to Meredith and Julia. "Y'all come with me now."

They followed the older lady as she walked through the foyer and past the grand staircase to the kitchen. As they walked along, Meredith glanced at Julia. "You were decidedly cool to that woman. What's the story?"

"We were close friends from grade school through high school," Julia said dismissively. "She went to UGA and I went to Georgia Southern. We grew apart."

"Uh-huh." Meredith's tone was disbelieving. "An ice cube would have been warmer than you were to her. What'd she do?"

Julia shrugged. "Let's just say she embraced the UGA sorority lifestyle. And that didn't include keeping gauche friends who weren't part of the old money set." She had to work to keep bitterness out of her tone. Funny, she hadn't realized this was still a tender spot after all these years. But in truth, she generally just avoided thinking about Gaye at all.

Meredith shot her a sympathetic glance. "It's hurtful when old friends get 'too good' for you, isn't it?"

Julia smiled gratefully at her friend. Meredith could easily have gone to the University of Georgia, but she'd chosen Georgia Southern, where she and Julia had met and become the best of friends. "It was at the time." She shrugged as they followed Miss Cora into a spacious, updated kitchen with gleaming stainless appliances and acres of black granite countertop.

A middle-aged woman in a pinafore-style apron was just setting a kettle on the large gas range as they entered. She then picked up a rolling pin to flatten dough on a section of the counter that had been liberally floured. A floury-fingerprinted juice glass stood nearby in lieu of a cookie cutter.

"Susan, I have guests," Miss Cora announced. "Will you please make tea for three and serve it in the parlor?"

"Yes, Miss Cora." The woman smiled at Julia and Meredith. "Y'all make sure she sits down and rests. She's had a busy day already."

"We will," Julia assured her, smiling.

"And make sure you put on your sweater first," Susan said to her employer, wagging a finger playfully. "It's chilly in here today."

It wasn't really chilly, but Julia knew elderly people often grew chilled even when temperatures were warm.

"Susan's my keeper," Miss Cora said, grinning an impish grin and winking. "She keeps me fed, makes sure I take my medicines, and keeps the house and my wardrobe in good condition."

"You're very blessed to have such a good housekeeper," Meredith said.

"She's been with us since we moved my mother in over twenty years ago. I don't know how I'd have gotten through my mother's passing in 2012 and then losing Jasper two years ago without her." Miss Cora led the way through another door into a long room that must have served as a family room, where a huge Christmas tree dominated a space before the front window and a fire of gas logs danced merrily in the fireplace. Weak winter sunlight streamed through sheer curtains that covered the windows even though the elaborate window treatments of heavier drapes were pulled back. The older lady gestured to some chairs near the tree. "Please have a seat," she requested. "I'd better put on my sweater. I don't dare disobey Susan."

She headed for what was clearly her favorite chair, a chocolate leather recliner with an afghan folded across the back and a table with magazines, a drink coaster, and the television remote neatly arranged beside it. A basket of knitting sat beneath it, a baby's cap lying on top that looked nearly complete.

Donning a sweater that had been tossed across the arm of the chair, Miss Cora sank carefully into the recliner and raised her footrest. "Make yourselves comfortable, and don't mind me," she told the partners, waving her hand. "Susan's right. I've been on my feet a bit much today. When she brings the tea in, we'll talk business."

As they waited for the refreshments, Miss Cora quizzed Meredith and Julia about the agency, recent cases they'd solved, and whether they were enjoying their "little venture," as she called it. "I always thought it would be fun to have a career," she told them, pronouncing it, "cah-REE-ah," in the accent of a true Southerner. "But of course women of means did not work when I was a young woman." She rolled her eyes, intimating what she thought of those strictures. "Our job was to keep the home nice, care for the children, and raise funds for various civic organizations."

Julia was amused to note the use of the word "funds" rather than "money." With true upper-crust Southern gentility, Miss Cora would probably never let such a common word pass her lips.

Susan appeared a moment later, wheeling a tea cart with a two-tiered platter of holiday cookies and other goodies, creamer, sugar, lemon wedges, and a pretty ceramic pot of steeping tea. She maneuvered the cart into the free space at one side of Miss Cora's chair and efficiently began to prepare the older woman's tea. Then she did the same for Meredith and Julia.

Miss Cora waved a piece of paper folded into quarters that she had picked up from the table beside her. "And while we have our little treats, I'll explain why I'd like to hire you."

Meredith paused in the act of reaching for her tea. "You want to hire us?"

Miss Cora nodded. "I believe I do."

"What for?" Julia blurted.

"I need you to find out more about the children in this picture," the elderly lady said simply. She passed Julia the square of paper she'd been holding.

Intensely curious, Julia carefully unfolded the single sheet of paper. Photocopied on the top half was a newspaper photo with a caption beneath. Below that was a blown-up image showing a close-up of just the people in the middle of the picture.

Meredith craned her neck to see, so Julia angled the piece of paper. The photo, top and bottom, was of five children. Two boys, two girls, and an infant whose gender was indeterminate, held in the arms of the biggest child, a boy. In the top picture, the five sat on the stoop of a rickety-looking porch that fronted a run-down shack. Around the edges, stretching in every direction, were fields of some tall-growing crop. Corn or sorghum, Julia thought. It was impossible to tell.

The caption beneath the top photograph read: *"Five Children for Sale. Five children in rural Guyton, Georgia, will be sold or given away by their widowed mother, who can no longer care for them."* A handwritten date in the top right corner read 7/14/35.

Meredith recoiled. "Oh, that's awful! How sad."

Julia nodded, looking away from the disturbing picture. "Who are these children?"

Miss Cora shrugged. "I have no idea. That's what I'm hoping you can tell me."

"Where did you get this?" Meredith asked.

Miss Cora sighed. "I found it in my mother's Bible. My mama passed away eight years ago at one hundred and four. Can you believe that?" She shook her head. "I was curious about this at the time, and I put in it a safe place, but we had funeral arrangements to make and out-of-town family coming, and then her estate to deal with, and I forgot about it for a bit. And then…" She shrugged, looking sheepish. "I couldn't remember where I'd put it for safekeeping." She grinned. "It was really safe, wasn't it?"

Meredith chuckled. "Apparently."

"Turned out I put it in a little safe with my will," Miss Cora told them. "This week I decided to take a look at the will to make sure it still reflected my wishes, and lo and behold, there was the picture."

"It doesn't say what newspaper this came from," Julia pointed out. "But I guess we could start by checking newspaper archives."

"Miss Cora?" Meredith hesitated for a moment. "Do you have any thoughts about who these children could be? Did your parents ever mention anything that might give us an idea?"

The elderly lady shook her head. "My mama never said a word about anything to do with a picture like this. I was an only child. I had a few older cousins but no one close to my age around very much."

"Could your mother have known the family somehow?"

Miss Cora hesitated. "Maybe? But I doubt it. We lived up in Buckhead when I was born and for the first few years of my life. My mother never spoke much about those years. She wasn't much for socializing. In any case, I can't imagine how she'd have known a poor family from rural Georgia."

Julia couldn't imagine it, either. Buckhead was an affluent sub-urb northwest of Atlanta that was a wooded and secluded enclave for the extremely wealthy long before it was annexed to the city.

"We moved back to Savannah, where both sets of my grandpar-ents lived, when I was about three and a half," Miss Cora added.

Julia leaned forward, covering Miss Cora's hand with one of her own. "Thank you for trusting us with this search," she said. "We'll do our very best to find out who these children are."

"Thank you," Miss Cora said. She turned her hand up and squeezed Julia's. "I have never mentioned this—the picture—to my children. I don't want to worry them. Can we keep this just between us girls?"

Julia smiled. "Absolutely. Anything you share with us will be kept completely confidential, Miss Cora."

"Just between us girls," echoed Meredith, leaning in to hug the old woman. "May we take this with us?" she asked, indicating the paper. "We'll just make a copy and return it to you."

"Oh, we don't need to do that," Julia said. "I'll just take a picture with my phone, and we can scan it into our files."

After she angled the photo for the best light and got several images of it, Julia took Miss Cora's hand. "We'll be in touch as soon as we have any information to share."

"That would be fine," Miss Cora said. "I'll let y'all go now. Susan will show you out while I have a little snooze here in my chair." She rang a silver bell beside her chair, and Susan came into the room at once.

After thanking her for the tea, Meredith and Julia took their leave. All the homes and inns on the Holiday Tour were downtown, and the partners were not far from their office on Whitaker Street along Forsyth Park, where Julia had parked. As they walked west along Gaston Street, Meredith pulled out her cell phone again.

"I just checked our email, and we have a potential new client," she told Julia.

"What's the case like?" Julia kept an eye on the uneven sidewalk as she dodged a trailing bit of Spanish moss, grateful she had worn comfortable flats with good arch support today.

"Workman's comp fraud," Meredith summarized, stepping around a clump of moss that lay on the sidewalk. "The owner of the company would like to speak with us about an employee he thinks is faking."

Julia nodded. "Great. We'll start Monday morning with two new cases." And one of them would be tricky and unusual, she thought, wondering yet again how the children in the old newspaper photo could have been connected to Miss Cora's mother.

Chapter Two

"OH, I FORGOT TO TELL YOU," Meredith said as they walked along the edge of Forsyth Park. "I invited Quin to be my escort for the Penny's Place gala."

"That's great!" Julia was pleased. Arthur "Quin" Crowley, an attorney, was someone both she and her husband Beau liked immensely. "Want to go together?"

"I'd love to," Meredith said. "I like Quin, but I'd feel better going with y'all and keeping it a bit more casual. But my other option was to ask Chase, and frankly, I'm sure he's getting tired of escorting his mother every time she calls." She referred to her younger son, who lived and worked in Atlanta but usually came home at least once a month.

Julia chuckled. "When's he coming home again?"

Meredith shrugged. "He hasn't said, but I assume he'll be here for Christmas as usual. I'll invite everyone to my house for our little Christmas Eve party."

Ever since the friends had renewed their close relationship when Julia moved back to Savannah fifteen years ago, the women and their families and a few other friends had gotten together for an early supper before church, and oftentimes they'd continued the party after services had concluded. Meredith usually played hostess, but for the past two years, Julia had done so while her friend was still struggling after Ron's passing and her own unexpected heart attack. Julia was happy to see that Meredith felt ready to step up to hosting again this year.

They walked around to the back of the agency and got into Julia's car. She had offered to drop Meredith at her home a few blocks away before heading southeast to her own home out along Herb River.

"Are you guys still up for joining me, Carmen, and the kids for the light show at the Botanical Gardens tonight?" Meredith asked, as Julia paused at the corner of Habersham and East Charlton Streets beside Meredith's historic home. She pulled to the curb to allow a horse-drawn carriage bearing tourists to pass her.

"Absolutely," Julia told her. Meredith's older son, Carter, and his family were coming and would stay overnight. Carter and Sherri Lynn were attending a holiday party at a friend's home in town while Meredith planned to take the children to see the light display. "Beau read that they have over a million lights this year, and I swear he's planning on counting to see if they're right. I'm wearing sneakers tonight. My feet are telling me comfort is more important than style."

Meredith laughed. "Mine are shouting the same thing. Oh, and Carmen is meeting us there." Carmen Lopez was their agency receptionist, office assistant, and general girl Friday, capable of managing three tasks at a time while still smiling at a client. Julia and Meredith adored her. Carmen rented a house just off Anderson Street near Savannah Classical Academy, and she would never allow them to pick her up at her home. Julia knew the area was among the less savory in town, and she often wished they could do more to help the young woman, who often struggled to make ends meet.

"Sounds like a plan." Julia waved as Meredith hopped out of the vehicle.

"Thanks for the ride. See you after my nap." Meredith waved before heading up the steps of her home.

***

"This is so beautiful!" Carmen paused before the columned front porch of the Coastal Georgia Botanical Gardens' education center building and drank in the decor. Lights. Poinsettias. White furniture. Red bows. Julia stopped beside their young friend, taking in the sights from the viewpoint of someone who had never been there before, as Carmen freely admitted she hadn't.

The gardens were located ten miles southwest of downtown Savannah on an old bamboo farm, but they were easily reached since the Truman Parkway had been completed a few years before, connecting the upper part of the city to Route 204 just below where Abercorn Street merged with it. It was a perfect evening, just under sixty degrees. Julia had donned a deep red fleece with a Christmassy scarf in green, red, and sparkling silver, along with black slacks and sturdy sneakers.

Garland strung with lights festooned the railings and wreaths, while holiday centerpieces and rocking chairs adorned the porch. Spread out for acres behind the building were dozens of lighted displays. Some highlighted the many gorgeous plants in the gardens, while others, such as a host of angels trumpeting news of the birth of the Child, were created with frames.

"I love this place," Meredith said. "And not just at Christmas, although I have to say this gets more amazing each year. I think my favorite time to visit is when all the bearded irises are in bloom in the spring."

"Christmas is my favorite," Julia declared as the pair followed Beau, Carmen, and Meredith's grandchildren through the covered porch out into the gardens. "I've just accepted I'm a crow. If it's shiny and sparkly, it makes me happy."

They wandered in the same general direction as many of the other guests, passing large Christmas trees decorated with strands of lights and huge, lighted flowers shaped to look like white poinsettias.

"This is a very nice display." Meredith's ten-year-old grandson, Kaden, dropped back to walk with them.

Julia suppressed a chuckle. Kaden's logical, orderly mind rarely veered toward superlatives. His red hair and freckles often made him look fun-loving and cheerful, but he rarely had spontaneous moments. "Coming from you, that's high praise," she said. "Look ahead. Don't you think those illuminated trees are gorgeous?"

Kaden considered the trees, which were spotlighted from below in shades of red, green, purple, and blue, making the branches stand out in colorful relief. "Yes," he said. "I believe 'gorgeous' is an appropriate term for those."

Resisting the urge to ruffle his hair, Julia smiled and was gratified when he leaned into her for a moment. "I'm glad you're enjoying it." Along with an inability to understand humor or teasing, Kaden generally didn't care to be touched casually.

Kaden cast a backward glance at the path along which they'd traveled. "I estimate that so far we have seen approximately two hundred thousand lights. I didn't count them individually."

"Only eight hundred thousand to go," Julia said cheerfully, grinning at him as they approached an arbor festooned with a unique display of lights in the shape of clusters of purple grapes and green-lit leaves. "Onward and upward."

As they came out of the arbor, her eyes were dazzled by dozens of displays in the heart of the gardens. "Which way should we go, Grandma?" Kaden's younger sister, Kinsley, asked, bouncing along beside Carmen.

"Your choice," Meredith responded.

"That way." Kinsley pointed toward the right-hand path that led past a little structure that they all knew sold hot chocolate. Julia hung back to take a picture with her phone. Just as she pressed the button, she caught sight of a familiar face on a path not far from theirs. Meredith's younger son, Chase, was strolling arm in arm with a leggy brunette in white pants and a short denim jacket over a longer denim shirt in a lighter blue hue.

Julia almost called out to him to come say hello to his mother, but Meredith had disappeared into the snack bar with Beau and the kids. Besides, he was a bit far away for Julia to be screaming like a fishwife just to get his attention when he was clearly engrossed in a conversation. His head was bent close to the shining mane of the woman's hair, and she walked close to his side.

Well! Julia didn't recognize the young woman, but she'd spent a lot of years away from Savannah, so that wasn't surprising. But she'd been under the distinct impression that Chase was a free agent. And there was also the fact that she was pretty certain Meredith had no idea he was in town.

She turned, frowning a bit, to follow the others.

Carmen stood outside the door of the snack shack, her dark eyes wide with shock as she stared at Chase and the woman. Julia knew Chase had shown interest in Carmen, just as she knew Carmen had had a few well-hidden dreams of a certain Prince Charming Bellefontaine.

Carmen's eyes met Julia's at that instant, and in them, Julia read disappointment, pride, hurt, and a whole host of other emotions. With a toss of her raven hair, Carmen whirled and vanished into the building, while Julia followed more slowly. What in the world was Chase doing in Savannah? And why hadn't he told his mother he'd be coming?

As she entered the brightly lit interior of the snack bar, her gaze scanned the picnic tables until she found her group just settling down with hot chocolate and a variety of tasty treats.

Carmen was paying for her own drink up at the counter. She didn't look at Julia as she turned and headed for the table.

Julia bit her tongue, resisting the urge to ask Carmen if she was all right. Sympathy would surely be rejected. After getting her own drink and a giant white chocolate and macadamia nut cookie that she couldn't resist, she joined Beau and their friends, sliding into a seat beside Kaden.

"So, what do you think so far?" she asked him.

"Did you know these gardens are fifty-one acres big?" he asked her earnestly.

"Wow. That's a lot of walking," she said, grinning at him.

He tilted his head, frowning. "But this light display doesn't cover all fifty-one acres."

"Thank goodness!" She chuckled. Trust Kaden to take her statement literally. Looking across the table at Meredith, she said, "I thought I saw Chase outside."

"Oh, you must not have seen right." Meredith barely looked up from her hot chocolate. "He'd have called if he was coming to town. Wouldn't it have been fun if he'd joined us?"

Julia risked a glance at Carmen, seated at the far end of the picnic table. She was glaring ferociously into her hot chocolate as if she'd found something objectionable in its depths. "Maybe I was wrong," Julia said aloud. But in her heart of hearts, she knew what she'd seen. And Carmen had seen him too.

***

Julia drove up the Truman and headed into town on Henry Street Monday morning, singing along as her radio blared out Tommy Dorsey's arrangement of "Sentimental Journey." Turning right on Drayton, she skirted the top end of Forsyth, turned left on Gaston, and crossed Whitaker, the street on which the agency was located. Easing into her parking space, she could see that Carmen and Meredith both had arrived before her.

She entered the building from the back, calling a cheery "Good morning!"

"Good morning," Meredith called from her office at the front of the building.

"Morning." That was Carmen, also up front.

In her own office that overlooked the small courtyard behind the building, Julia hung the flared cape she'd worn on a hook behind the door. She withdrew her leather-bound planner from the large bag she carried and placed it on her desk beside her keyboard. Then she withdrew a cooler of snacks she'd brought along for the week and took those to the kitchen, where she picked up the mug she'd washed on out Friday.

Carrying the mug to the coffee station, she called, "Thanks for starting the coffee," to the other two. She didn't know who'd done it, nor did she care. She was just grateful it was there, and smiled to herself as she inhaled the steam that rose as she poured her first cup.

After returning to her office, she booted up her computer and unzipped her planner. Although she was fully capable of keeping her life organized digitally, Julia enjoyed the act of hand writing items in her planner, of keeping her tasks, her to-do list, and her daily notes there and transferring items to her computer files. She found it helped her cement them in her brain.

She glanced at the clock. Almost nine thirty. She and Meredith generally met every Monday to review cases and make their plans for the week, unless one of them had an early appointment. She picked up her planner and her coffee, then she left her office and walked along the hall to the front of the building.

Carmen was at her desk, busily hammering away at her keyboard without ever taking her eyes off the monitor. "Meredith's waiting for you," she said.

"I know." Julia smiled. "Did you have a good Sunday?"

Carmen shrugged, pausing in her typing. "I've had better." Her tone was glum and resigned.

"Oh no. What's wrong?" Julia set her mug down and waited expectantly.

Meredith, hearing the question, had popped her head out of her office. "Anything we can help with?"

Carmen shook her head. "No. Just the same old, same old. My clothes dryer gave up the ghost yesterday." She shrugged, and there was an edge of defiance in it. "I'm hoping it can be patched up, but no big deal if it can't. I'll just go to the laundromat."

It was a bigger deal than Carmen wanted to let on, Julia knew. When Carmen had rented her little house, the washer and dryer were included, but there was a stipulation in her contract that if they stopped working, the landlord was not responsible for replacing them. Neither was Carmen, which had seemed a good thing at the time. Now, not so much. There were times of day when it was safer than others to use many of the laundromats around town. Unfortunately, Carmen worked during those hours. It was most definitely not safe for a young woman to be in such a place in the evening hours. And that left weekend days, which meant leaving everything else she wanted to get done and sitting with her laundry for some of those precious all-too-short leisure hours.

Julia's heart sank. "I'm so sorry," she said. It felt terrifically inadequate.

Meredith was shaking her head. "You can't go to the laundromat, especially in the evening. You can use mine. The laundry room is right inside the back door, and you already have a key. I promise not to bug you about work. You could come and go as you pleased. You wouldn't have to sit and wait for it like you would at the laundromat."

Carmen's relief was all over her face. "Oh, Meredith, are you sure it wouldn't be any trouble?"

Meredith looked at Julia. "You'll be saving me hours of worrying about you." She clasped her hands dramatically. "Please, Carmen, for my sake."

Carmen laughed. "Well, when you put it that way…I accept." She rushed to Meredith and hugged her. "And thank you."

Laughing, Julia picked up her coffee mug, and the partners crossed the hall to Meredith's office. Meredith occupied the small floral couch, where she already had her laptop and a sea of notes spread out around her, while Julia chose one of the nearby wingback chairs and laid her planner in her lap.

"Okay," Meredith said, "we've got a couple of things to add to our existing agenda for this week."

"Miss Cora's case and the possible worker's comp fraud." Julia listed them on her fingers.

"Oh, and by the way," Meredith said, "that probably was Chase you saw on Saturday evening. He came down to visit old friends and showed up late at my house. He joined me for church and lunch on Sunday before driving back to Atlanta."

"How nice," Julia said, drawing out the word. She was hyper-aware that Carmen in the outer room could surely hear every word. She made a show of consulting her planner. "So, let's talk about these new jobs. You go first."

Meredith nodded, looking through her glasses at her laptop. "I don't have details yet," she said, "but I called the owner this morning, and he's coming by at eleven to speak with us about it. He has an employee claiming worker's compensation who he thinks might be faking the injury."

Julia made notes. "Sounds like it might be stakeout time."

Meredith chuckled "You might be right. I think the thing I enjoy most about surveillance is that absolutely no one suspects either of us."

"Little old ladies, you mean," Julia said, grinning.

"I wouldn't go that far," Meredith protested. "But certainly sweet-looking senior Southern matrons."

"So, we'll meet with…" Meredith consulted the email she'd pulled up. "Kenny Swann is the owner. The business is called Swann Lawnscapes. They specialize in high-end residential landscaping, irrigation, and regular lawn care. Apparently, none of the employee's coworkers saw the incident she claims caused an ankle injury. The employee has threatened legal action."

"Hmm. I guess we can ask a few more questions, and then we'll need to learn more specifics about this woman so we can check her out," Julia said.

"Agreed. So, what do you make of this photo Miss Cora gave us?" Meredith asked. She laid the copy Carmen had printed face up on the coffee table between them.

"July fourteenth, nineteen thirty-five." Julia read the date again. "I have no earthly idea."

"I wonder if Miss Cora is one of those children," Meredith said.

"I wondered the same thing immediately, given her age," Julia added. "Some of those children would be very close to her age now. I think it's possible. But I also think we shouldn't get hung up on chasing a theory we don't have any evidence for. There could be other reasons her mother had that picture in her Bible."

"Maybe Miss Cora's parents wanted to adopt one of them," Meredith said.

"Also a good possibility," Julia said.

"But obviously they didn't, since Cora said she was an only child," Meredith recalled.

"Maybe they did, and the child didn't survive," Julia theorized. "Let's keep both of these possibilities in mind."

Meredith nodded. "I suppose the logical starting point would be to figure out where this photo was published."

"The *Savannah Morning News*," Julia said promptly. "That's my guess."

"Okay," Meredith said. "As soon as our eleven o'clock leaves, we'll get lunch and then start the search for this photo. Maybe there was an article or more information that gives the children's names."

Just then, the silvery sound of a small bell tinkled, signaling the opening of the front door. The women had debated whether or not a bell was tasteful or tacky, but in the end, practicality had won out. There were moments when none of them were right up front, and they didn't want someone to walk in unannounced and not be greeted.

Meredith and Julia both paused.

"Are you expecting anyone?" Meredith asked.

Julia shook her head. "You?"

"No." Meredith cocked her head, and Julia fell silent as they heard Carmen's voice welcoming their guest.

A moment later, a feminine voice said, "Is Ms. Foley in this morning?"

"Certainly. And who may I say has come to call?" Carmen's formality seemed to fit the house and the agency.

"Gaye Strieter. It's a business matter."

"Have a seat, Ms. Strieter," Carmen invited. "I'll see if Ms. Foley is available."

In Meredith's office, Julia's eyes widened. What on earth was Gaye Strieter doing here?

Chapter Three

A MOMENT LATER, CARMEN APPEARED in the doorway. She closed the door behind her and said, "There's a Gaye Strieter here for Julia. Sounds like she wants to talk about a case."

Julia looked at Meredith. "Want to take this one?"

But Meredith shook her head. "She specifically asked for you. She has a connection with you, however many years ago it was."

"I know." Julia heaved a sigh. She rose and set her planner on the chair, then mimed an exaggerated motion of someone pulling up her pants.

Carmen looked mystified. "What are you doing?"

Julia hooked a thumb at Meredith. "She basically just told me to put on my big girl pants." She sighed again and headed for the door. "So I did."

Carmen's expression lightened, and she giggled. As Julia opened the door, she looked back over her shoulder and winked at Carmen. Meredith, still on the sofa, gave her an encouraging thumbs-up, at which Julia stuck out her tongue before arranging her features into a pleasant smile and crossing the hallway to the reception area.

"Gaye. How nice to see you again. What brings you downtown today?"

"I-I'd like to speak with you about maybe taking me on as a client." Gaye looked incredibly nervous. She was dressed in trim navy slacks and a navy twinset. The cardigan bore burgundy and white Christmas ornaments trailing down the front, and she wore a Saint Laurent crossbody bag in dark red that matched her neat leather Stuart Weitzman flats. She looked like exactly what she was—a polished upper-crust Savannah mover and shaker.

Julia suppressed the adolescent flare of resentment that rose. She supposed that same appellation could be attached to her now, so she could hardly dislike it, could she?

"Why don't you follow me to my office, and we can chat?" Julia invited.

"We could walk over to the Bean and talk on the way," Gaye suggested. The Sentient Bean was a quaint little coffee shop at the southern end of Forsyth Park that was beloved by locals and tourists alike. It also was a hefty walk, which would force Julia to spend far more time in this woman's company than she had planned.

"I'm afraid I've got other appointments this morning, and I can't spare the time," Julia said. And that wasn't really even a lie. She *did* have other things to do this morning. "Would you like Carmen to bring you coffee or tea?"

"A little coffee would be nice, thank you," Gaye said, following Julia down the hallway.

"It'll be just a minute," Carmen said, emerging from Meredith's office.

Julia entered her office and gestured toward an arrangement of two carved French Louis XV chairs with needlepointed cushions. Between them stood an elegant piecrust table with a tall vase of lilies. Julia carried the lilies to the fireplace and set them on the mantel before joining her guest at the small table. "So how can Magnolia Investigations help you?" she asked, determined to keep this meeting as businesslike as possible.

"This is lovely," Gaye said, her eyes trailing along the seafoam green drapes that picked up colors in the needlepoint on the chairs, the green and white striped chaise before the fireplace flanked by a white wingback chair, and Julia's beloved desk that she'd used throughout her first career and had brought with her to her second.

"Thank you." Julia waited.

"I've imagined sitting here together—sitting anywhere together—sharing a cup of coffee for a long time," Gaye said. "We used to be such good friends, didn't we?"

Julia glanced pointedly at her watch. She was *not* going to get drawn into fond reminiscences of days gone by. "That was a very long time ago."

Carmen breezed in, carrying a tea tray. She set a cup of coffee in front of Gaye, off-loaded sugar, creamer, and even a small plate of petit fours, as well as Julia's mug that she'd left in Meredith's office. "There you go," she said. "Let me know if there's anything else you need."

"I think we're fine, thank you." Julia smiled at Carmen, who nodded and left the room.

"Goodness, she's efficient. I think I'm a bit afraid of her," Gaye commented.

That startled a laugh from Julia. "We all are," she assured her guest. Then, remembering this was not a social call, she prompted, "You said you may want to hire us?"

Gaye sighed, appearing to recognize that there was to be no small talk. "I think so." She opened the classy purse and took out a photograph. "I want you to check into my son-in-law."

Julia took the picture that had obviously been printed from a color printer. "Why?"

"It's possible he may be cheating on my daughter."

Julia wasn't sure what she'd expected, but this certainly wasn't it. "What, uh, what makes you think that?"

Gaye waved a hand. "Lots of little things. They have young children, and she's busy with them every minute of the day. And of course, she's exhausted by the time they get them in bed. He works all the time, and they barely spend any time together."

"Sounds like a lot of young couples," Julia said. "A lot of people I know have said if your marriage survives the years of babies and toddlers, it can survive anything."

"I wish that were true." Gaye sounded sad. "You never had children, did you?"

Julia raised an eyebrow. That was a surprisingly personal question from someone she barely knew anymore. "No," she finally said. "I didn't." She didn't elaborate.

A tide of pink washed into Gaye's cheeks. "That was incredibly ill-mannered of me," she said. "Please accept my sincere apology."

"Accepted." Julia forced an ease into her tone that she didn't feel. Not one little bit. She stood, laying the photograph on the table. "If you're sure about this, I'll send Carmen in to get information on your son-in-law."

"Information like what?" Gaye's brow crinkled.

"His name, address, where he works, for starters," Julia said dryly. "And she'll set up an account for you and explain our billing process." She extended her hand. "Thank you for coming in. We'll endeavor to present you with as complete a report as possible."

After a brief handshake, she turned and left the room. It certainly wasn't usual procedure to have Carmen elicit important information from a client, but Julia did not feel able to spend one more moment in Gaye's company. They'd been such good friends as children. All through high school. They'd been inseparable the summer after graduation, and she could still remember their parting before they'd each headed off to their respective colleges. And then…

Nothing. There had been a few phone calls. Even fewer letters, which had been filled with Gaye's enthusiasm for all her new friends and the sorority she had rushed practically the moment she got on campus. She hadn't come home at Thanksgiving at all, and over the holiday break, when Julia had called, Gaye's mother had ever-so-genteelly and apologetically explained that Gaye had gone to Florida with friends the day after Christmas and wouldn't be back until time to return to school.

Those wonderful childhood memories hurt to recall now. It had been far easier to bury them over the decades since. If Magnolia Investigations could help Gaye with her son-in-law problem, they would. But Julia had no intention of pretending she was thrilled to see and spend time with an old friend.

After Gaye left, Julia finished up some items on her to-do list. Then she decided it was time for a little sleuthing. She pulled the copy of the newspaper photo out and began a search for the

Savannah Morning News archives. It would probably take only a few moments to find more information about the photo. Had there once been an article attached to it?

Fifteen minutes later, Julia growled in frustration. A bunch of dead ends was the only thing she had to show for her efforts. Almost all of the newspaper's searchable archives were geared toward genealogy. One had to know the names of the people one wanted to search for. The Digital Library of Georgia raised her hopes briefly, but the same problem occurred. The date bore no results, nor did "children for sale" or "five children" and variations along those lines. And those were nearly the only things she knew about the photo. A visit to the paper might be in order.

***

Promptly at eleven o'clock, a stocky, harried-looking man stepped through the door of Magnolia Investigations, just as Julia came toward Meredith's office from her own in preparation for their next client.

"Kenny Swann," he said when Carmen introduced herself and welcomed him. "I'm here to meet with somebody about a workman's comp case."

"We're expecting you," Carmen said.

Julia stepped forward and offered her hand. "I'm Julia Foley. Let's go across the hall into this office, and I'll introduce you to my partner."

As they walked into Meredith's office, Mr. Swann stopped abruptly. "Both of you are women?" he asked skeptically. "I thought there'd be at least one man involved in a detective agency."

Julia felt herself bristle, and she told herself to relax. Meredith smiled, and Julia hoped Mr. Swann didn't recognize the sharp glint of annoyance in her blue eyes. "We don't consider ourselves a detective agency, Mr. Swann. We do private, confidential investigations. We look into things when someone comes to us with a problem. Our job is to give you more information about your concern so you can make informed decisions. Now, you mentioned in your email that you have a former employee you believe doesn't really have the injury for which she's claiming workers' compensation. Is that correct?"

Her concise summation of the situation took some of the wind out of his sails.

"Yeah, that's right." He looked a bit sheepish. "And call me Kenny, okay?"

Meredith ushered him to a seat. "To begin with, let us tell you how we would go about proving your case. Or disproving it, as the case may be. We will not 'make up' or create evidence to support your position. What we will do is thoroughly investigate this employee, including the use of surveillance if necessary, and return a dossier of results to you. Is that acceptable?"

"I'm not asking you to do anything illegal," Kenny said. "Here's what happened. Two weeks ago, my receptionist, Hilly Pettis, called and told me she'd gone to her doctor after getting off work the day before, and she was going to have to file a workman's comp claim. Said she'd injured her ankle when she tripped over something that had fallen off a truck in the parking lot. The trouble is, none of the guys on the returning crew who were nearby saw it happen. But I can't prove it didn't, and Hilly got a doctor to certify that she was injured."

He fell silent, and Julia prompted, "But you suspect she wasn't."

Kenny nodded. "It just seems fishy. Her sister is getting married next year, and she asked me for time off to go dress shopping and look for reception venues and all this stuff." He waved a hand in the air, clearly not seeing the importance of these events. "But the problem is, she's out of her paid time off for the year, and I really need her in the office, so I told her that wouldn't work for me. And the next thing you know, she pops up with this injury and has a doctor say she can't work for a month." He took off the gimme cap with the company's logo emblazoned on it and ran a hand through his unruly brown hair. "Doctor's note says she must be resting with the foot raised and that she can't work. Period. If she's really hurt, I'll be the last one to complain. If she got hurt while she was on our property, I won't say another word. But I got a funny feeling about this, you know?"

"So you contacted us," Meredith concluded. "It sounds as if you need someone to do some quiet investigating." She gestured to Julia. "We were just saying this morning that no one ever suspects us of conducting surveillance because we look so harmless."

The landscaper actually smiled, revealing even white teeth and an engaging grin. "Now, *that* I can believe. So, you'd...watch her? With, like, a camera?"

"Exactly," Meredith said. "That would certainly be one of the major steps we would take. Did you examine the doctor's information?"

Kenny nodded. "The guy practices right here in Savannah. He's an ER doc at St. Joseph's/Candler." He named one of the city's two largest hospitals. "I guess maybe that's where she went when she thought she was hurt. I dunno."

"Did you ask to see Hilly's medical records?"

Kenny shifted in his seat. "Yeah, but they didn't mean a whole lot to me, and let me tell you, hiring a medical firm to review them and probably order more medical tests and stuff is about the most expensive way to go about this I can think of. When you emailed me back about your rates, I thought maybe we could try this first."

"We'd like to see any paperwork you have, including the medical records," Julia told him. "And we'll need any information you have about this employee, particularly her full name, photograph or description, and address."

"If you think you'd like to have us pursue this, that is," Meredith said smoothly.

Kenny nodded. "Yeah, yeah, I would. Can you start tomorrow?"

Meredith smiled at him. "We can start today. Let me have our assistant prepare a contract, and we can review it."

***

The partners left Carmen to handle the office and left for a quick lunch break at Green Truck, a fabulous neighborhood pub on Habersham just a few blocks north of Ardsley Park, the premier midtown neighborhood just south of Victory Drive. Green Truck, named for the old mint-green Chevy that slouched outside the entry, was renowned for its burgers as well as its vegetarian options. Julia, who'd driven, found a parking spot right in front of the building.

Meredith ordered a salad with spiced nuts, Gorgonzola cheese, apples, balsamic caramelized onions, and dried cranberries splashed with a balsamic vinaigrette dressing. She was careful, Julia noted, ever since her heart attack, about her diet and nutrition.

Julia herself decided, after much deliberation, to have the Veggie Reuben, a veggie patty on rye with Swiss cheese, sauerkraut, and Thousand Island dressing, served with the pub's delectable fries. Her mouth practically watered just thinking about it.

Meredith sat back, smiling and swirling a spoon in her sweet tea. "Gracious! Three new cases since Saturday. We're on a roll."

Julia grinned, nodding at her friend's comment. "And now we've got to figure out our game plan for each one of them. As far as I'm concerned, Gaye Strieter's case is the least urgent priority. Kenny Swann's is probably the first one we need to address, and Miss Cora's is somewhere in the middle."

"I agree," Meredith said. "We already have Gaye's son-in-law's information, so we can set up a surveillance schedule, and we can do the same when we receive the rest of the case info from Kenny Swann. Hopefully Carmen will have received that by the time we get back. I already drafted some ideas for Miss Cora's search this morning while you were finishing the write-up of last week's concluded cases. First, we need to find out what paper published this photo."

"On July 14, 1935," Julia said, checking the note she'd put in her phone. She summarized her fruitless efforts to find information online earlier.

"I've been trying to call the *SMN* to ask about their archives, but then I saw on Facebook that they're having some trouble with the phones this morning, so I guess we'd better just drive out there." The *Savannah Morning News*, fondly abbreviated *SMN* by area residents, had been started in 1850 under the name *Daily Morning News*, and had operated almost continuously, mostly as the *Savannah Morning News*, ever since.

"We could start at the *SMN* after lunch. Sound okay to you?"

"Yes," Meredith said. "Curiosity is killing this cat. I can't stop thinking about that photo."

"Me neither." Julia nodded. "Let's indulge our curiosity, and when we get back this afternoon, we'll set up surveillance schedules for both of the other cases, if Kenny's gotten us information on his employee. We might be able to get started with that case later this afternoon if this newspaper search goes quickly."

After they finished their meal, they headed out to see what they could find in the local newspaper's archives. The building was unexpectedly charming, considering how modern it was. The paper had moved out of Savannah to the new location west of town sixteen years ago, bringing some of its iconic fixtures, such as a carved wood reception desk, with it. Outside, the paper's name was scrolled across the building above four large columns in the lavishly embellished font used on the banner, and the same logo was carved above the reception desk in the spacious entry.

But when they inquired at the desk, the receptionist regretfully informed them that they did not keep microfiche copies of past papers stored there, only the most recent years since the advent of digital technology. "You'll have to go to the Bull Street Library," she told them, referring to one of the Live Oaks branches of the library system that had been incorporated into the Pines Public Library system in 2018. "They have all the old *SMN* papers on microfilm in the Georgia Room."

So back they drove to Savannah. The Bull Street Library was a century-old stately neoclassical building in the heart of the Victorian District. As always, the parking lot looked packed, so they snagged a spot a block away on West Thirty-Sixth Street and strolled over. After mounting the wide, shallow steps, they entered the grand foyer and turned left into the Kaye Kole Genealogy and Local History Room, affectionately nicknamed the Georgia Room.

The partners were shown to a room containing microfilm readers and decades' worth of archives.

"Here we go," Meredith said, after locating the reel of film for the date in question. "I can't wait to learn more about these kids."

Julia's hopes were high as she sat down before the machine and set up the microfilm. But a few minutes later, she sat back in disappointment. "Rats. It wasn't in this issue."

"You're kidding." Meredith blew out a breath of exasperation. "I wonder if the date is off by a day or two."

Julia removed the film from the machine and restored it to its container. "I guess we keep looking. You want to check the days going forward and I'll check going back? Hopefully it's not more than a week off."

An hour later, they had reviewed the entire month before and the month after with no results. "It's not here," Meredith said. "Either it was published in another paper or the date is completely off. We need to stop."

"It's hard to imagine that someone would have written down the wrong date," Julia said as they walked back to the car.

"Maybe it wasn't a local paper at all," Meredith said glumly.

"But it sure looked like the land around here would have looked almost a century ago," Julia said. "I swear those were sorghum fields around the shack."

Meredith laughed. "You've just described the entire two hundred and fifty miles between here and Atlanta a hundred years ago, excluding the city of Macon."

Julia grimaced. "And back then, probably every small town in between had its own newspaper."

They both groaned.

"Let's try to narrow it down," Meredith said. "We know this photo wouldn't have been published in the *Tribune*. These are clearly white children." The *Tribune* was another Savannah paper. Originally titled the *Colored Tribune,* the paper focused on the city's African American community.

"Okay. Let's look at the counties closest to us and find out what newspapers would have been published in each of them in 1935." Julia held up two fingers. "We could start with Liberty and Bryan, and then Effingham if we don't strike gold in the first two."

"Sounds like a plan," Meredith said. "Oh, I just got a text. Hold on." She righted the phone that had been lying in her lax palm and tapped the screen. "It's from Carmen. She's received the information Kenny Swann promised us."

"Great," Julia replied. "We can get started on that surveillance."

Fifteen minutes later, they were back at the office. Always efficient, Carmen had created files of information for both the Swann case and Gaye Strieter's son-in-law. They included background checks, real estate, and contact information, and everything else she'd been able to uncover while they'd been out, along with the information shared by each of the clients.

"I guess we'd better spend a few hours on each of these," Meredith said. "Do you have a preference which one you'd rather pursue?"

Julia promptly reached for the file on Kenny Swann's employee. She had no desire to work on the Strieter case, and she suspected Meredith had deliberately given her an out. "I'll take this one." She looked at the file. "Hilda Pettis, or Hilly, as Kenny called her. She lives in Parkside." Parkside was a neighborhood of modest older homes adjacent to Daffin Park and Grayson Stadium, where the Savannah Bananas, formerly the Sand Gnats, played baseball. Julia had never been able to decide which name was worse.

She pursed her lips. "We'll have to be careful. There will be neighbors wondering why there's a lady just sitting in her car." Apartment complexes were much easier for them, usually. "It's a corner lot, though, so that gives us plenty of options. Where's the other one?"

Meredith was flipping through her file. "The Crescent." She referred to a midtown neighborhood just east of Habersham Street that was listed on the National Register of Historic Places. The homes were gracious and generally well maintained. And costly. Some of the larger ones still had carriage houses on the properties.

Julia wondered what Gaye's son-in-law did. Houses in the Ardsley Park-Chatham Crescent area were not inexpensive, even when they were in dire need of renovation, as some of them were. "That'll be easier to surveil," she decided. "Lots of household help and lawn maintenance trucks coming and going. We should be able to blend in."

Meredith grinned. "I'm good at blending." She consulted her file again. "According to this, he works days at the hospital and drives a late-model black BMW SUV. I'm going to take a spin over there and see if I can locate it in the parking lot. If so, I'll try to park nearby and tail him when he leaves." She turned toward her office. "I'm going to gather my things and head home after I finish keeping an eye on this guy, whether it's at the hospital or elsewhere. While I'm watching, I'll work on a two-person schedule for each of them for the rest of the week."

"Sounds good," Julia said. "I'll do a preliminary survey of Hilly Pettis's home area. Maybe I'll get lucky and lay eyes on her."

Chapter Four

Parting ways with her friend, Julia entered her own office and gathered her things. She also picked up their camcorder, just in case she really did lay eyes on her subject. Designed to far exceed HD resolution, the little Sony captured excellent night shots and could produce excellent still images too. At this time of year, when the sun set at the same time many people got off work, it was invaluable. Meredith, she suspected, would have taken their digital camera so she could get some still shots.

After calling farewell to Carmen, who would lock up the office at five, Julia climbed back into her car and headed south on Whitaker Street until she could turn left on Anderson. Instead of hopping on the Truman to take her home, though, she drove south on Bee Road, crossing beneath the Truman. She passed Grayson Stadium and Daffin Park on her right, finally turning right onto Fifty-First Street and driving at a snail's pace along the residential street. Homes here were small and usually one- or two-story single-bath homes, many built almost a century ago. Julia drove slowly past small brick homes with porticos across the front, traditional-looking frame homes with small porches, steep front steps, and driveways that ran back to detached garages, ancient live oaks dripping with moss, and sago palms with their razor-sharp fronds.

Noting the house numbers, she felt her pulse quicken as she approached the intersection with Cedar Street. "There you are," she murmured to herself. The single-story frame house sat on a brick foundation on a small rise. A cement sidewalk led to a set of brick steps that preceded a small peak-covered stoop before the front door. The exterior was covered in soft blue-gray shingles, and although its windows boasted no storm shutters, it looked in good repair. A single-wide cement driveway ran along the right side of the house, stopping at a six-foot high wooden fence with lattice trim at the top. She wondered if it enclosed the entire backyard.

She slowed as she approached the corner. Window blinds were closed, preventing any view into the house, and there were no cars parked either in the driveway or before the house.

She slowly rounded the corner and drove around the side of the house, where presumably the one or two bedrooms were located. As she'd suspected, the fence enclosed the backyard. She turned right into the alley that ran between the homes on Fifty-First and Fifty-Second, which the garbage and recycling vehicles used, and which allowed homeowners with garages or back parking to access those. The house on the corner had no garage, only a closed gate that allowed the residents to access the alley. There would be little opportunity for observing her quarry from the back.

She continued down the alley, then drove up to Fifty-Second, went two blocks down, and cut over to drive down Fifty-First the other way. After she found a parking spot along the street, she cut the engine and picked up her phone, pretending to look at it while she surveyed the Pettis home, which was now ahead of her on the far left corner of the street.

It had been a pleasant day, and Julia rolled her window partially down to take advantage of the cool air as day slid toward evening. She glanced through the file as she watched the house.

Hilly Pettis was thirty-four years old. She was married. Her spouse worked for the City of Savannah, and they had two children, both of whom attended Jacob G. Smith Elementary about a mile away. It was one of the best public schools in the city, which drove up the price of even modest homes like this one. Five years ago, prior to going to work for Swann Lawnscapes, Hilly had worked for the City of Savannah in their Financial Services department on Bay Street. Maybe that was how she had met her husband, Julia mused.

She called Beau to let him know she'd be home by six at the latest. Just as she ended the call, a compact car came down Fifty-First and pulled into the driveway of the little blue house. A man got out of the car. He wore a pair of khakis with a white sport shirt with a logo over the heart, and Julia imagined this probably was the husband, home after a day at work. Two kids piled out of the back, lugging backpacks half the size they were. Julia raised the video camera, zoomed in closer, and began recording the scene. The wide-angle lens ensured she would miss nothing.

Then the door of the house opened. A woman on crutches appeared, maneuvering awkwardly onto the small stoop. The smaller child, a boy, ran toward her. She set one crutch aside, bent, and hugged him. Then she gave him a quick tickle, and he shrieked and giggled. Julia could hear it all the way from her car half a block away before the child darted past her into the house. The bigger child, a girl with an eye-watering backpack in hot pink and orange, gave her a hug before heading indoors. The man walked up the driveway and gave the woman a hug before holding the door so she could retrieve her crutch. A quick blare of a horn told Julia the man had locked the car before the couple walked into the house.

"Hmm," she said thoughtfully, lowering the camera. "Nothing unusual there." She was going to have to read through all the medical mumbo jumbo in the file very carefully to see exactly what type of injury Hilly Pettis had sustained and how long she expected to be on crutches.

***

The following day was Tuesday, and by the end of it, Julia was glad she had gotten the video of Hilly Pettis the evening before, because the woman didn't come out of the house at all during the time Julia was watching in the late morning and through the lunch hour.

"You're back," Meredith said as Julia entered the office.

"I am," Julia conceded. "With nothing to show for my hours of observation. Want to drive out to Hinesville with me?"

"I'd love to," Meredith said. "I've been going over accounts this morning and updating our website. I need to do something fun."

Julia laughed. "I'm not sure rooting through microfilm in a library qualifies as fun."

"It will be if we find that photo," Meredith predicted.

They said goodbye to Carmen and headed out to the little parking lot. Meredith got behind the wheel of her car, and Julia slid into the passenger seat, fastening her seat belt as Meredith put the car in reverse and backed onto Howard Street.

"So I didn't even catch a glimpse of my guy last night," Meredith said. "Either I was parked near the wrong BMW, or he was at work late. It was still parked there when I left at six. I hope you've had some better luck."

"I did." Julia told her about getting video of Hilly Pettis crouching down to hug the backpack-wearing child. "This morning was much less exciting. I never saw her once."

"That's not helpful," Meredith said. "What exactly is wrong with her?"

"I'm not sure. Kenny just said something about her foot or ankle, right? I need to read the doctor's diagnosis and treatment plan."

Meredith laughed. "And even then, we might not know what we're looking at." She sobered. "But we should, at the very least, be able to see what type of limitations she has."

Julia looked at the navigation screen in front of them as they cruised west along Gaston Street to Montgomery. From there, the highways would take them west to Garden City and then south and west to Hinesville, a small city that was the county seat. Hinesville was largely famous for its proximity to Fort Stewart, the largest army post in size in the eastern part of the country.

"I had a little time to research this morning," Meredith told her as they cruised down Interstate 95. "And I got just as frustrated as you were yesterday. The *Liberty County Herald* archives are not online, as far as I could tell. The paper operated from sometime in the 1800s to 1980, when it merged into the *Coastal Courier*. There are some scattered copies available in the University of Georgia archives, but 1935 wasn't listed as one. So, I called the *Courier* to confirm that they have archives, and they told me all the old ones are on microfilm at the library in Hinesville."

The Hinesville Library was another branch of the Live Oaks public library system. The collection had moved into a new building a few years ago, a long, low white block structure with a hint of neo-classical features and double front columns that made it look older than it actually was.

Meredith parked, and the friends entered the library. Julia felt the immediate familiarity that one who knew and enjoyed libraries felt, entering the hushed atmosphere where booklovers lurked amid the stacks, engrossed in the printed matter. Once again, they made a beeline for the history room, where the old *Liberty County Herald* newspapers were stored on microfilm.

Initially, their hopes were high, but after threading the microfilm into the reader and reviewing the date in question, Julia knew another crushing disappointment.

"It feels like the movie *Groundhog Day*," she grumbled, looking up from the microfilm reader. "Nothing on July 14, 1935."

Meredith sighed. "So, we'll look at the dates on either side of it again. But I'm not optimistic."

The pair suited actions to her words, but after an hour, it was clear that the photograph had not been published in the spring or summer of 1935 in the *Liberty County Herald*.

"Let's try Effingham County next," Meredith reminded Julia. "And then branch out to Bryan, Long, and some of the others farther away if we need to."

"I don't have a good feeling about this," Julia said. "What if we never find out who these people are?"

Meredith chuckled. "It's too early to get discouraged, my friend. This is only our second stop. Let's plan to go out to Effingham County as soon as we can fit it in."

***

On Wednesday, surveillance of their two most recent cases tied up one or the other of the partners for much of the day. It was largely fruitless, with neither Gaye's son-in-law nor Hilly Pettis being sighted. Knowing Meredith would want to be involved in the search to identify the children in Miss Cora's photograph, Julia confined her search for the identities of the children to more online research when she finally had time to pursue it late in the afternoon. It was another futile effort. Of all the things that had been digitized and uploaded to the internet in the past couple of decades, apparently community newspapers ranked low on the list of important documents.

So Thursday morning, after taking care of essential work like updating files and checking email, the partners headed out of the city yet again in search of the elusive photograph's origins. This time, they drove northwest to Effingham County, the final county that shared a border with Chatham County. Effingham also bordered South Carolina, separated from the neighboring state by the Savannah River.

Julia's research had revealed that the Springfield Lowcountry Historical Society held microfiche records of the now-defunct *Springfield Herald* all the way back to its first printing in 1890. Springfield was the county seat of Effingham County.

The historical society was a sprawling frame house on a raised brick foundation, the better to keep the house cool and prevent damp beneath it. The yard was enclosed within a simple iron fence and surrounded by mature hardwoods and shrubbery. Built in the Folk Victorian style, it featured a wide front porch with pretty spindle work around the eaves and decorative porch supports. There were also patterned shingles in the gables, and a small balcony overhung the first floor above the door.

Inside, the lone volunteer told them the house had been built in 1910 and refurbished for its present purpose a decade ago. She explained the climate control system that protected the many antiques, fragile fabrics, and books housed within, then she showed them to the microfilm collection off the foyer in a high-ceiling room with original wood floors.

By now, threading the microfilm through the machine and scrolling through the pages that came into view was a familiar routine. Julia took the reel for July of 1935 and quickly moved to the fourteenth. Her heart no longer raced with excitement. Repeated disappointments had shown her the difficulty of trying to find an image that was nearly a century old. It was quite likely, she knew, that the photograph had been taken somewhere farther away. An awful lot of southeastern Georgia had once been devoted to cotton, corn, sorghum, and other crops, and it could have been any county. Georgia had the dubious distinction of having the second most counties in the nation after Texas. Probably at least half of them had once held corn or sorghum fields—

"Meredith!" Her voice was hushed but urgent enough to capture her friend's attention where she stood scrolling through something on her phone.

"Tell me you found it," Meredith said in a fervent undertone, stashing her phone and clasping her fingers tightly together. The hush of the library discouraged loud voices or bigger expressions of excitement.

"I found it!" Julia leaned closer to the screen. It was undeniably the same photograph, albeit of slightly better quality than Miss Cora's grainy copy. The caption showed the same words, nothing more, nothing less. *"Five Children for Sale. Five children in rural Guyton, Georgia, will be sold or given away by their widowed mother, who can no longer care for them."*

But there was nothing else. Julia had harbored a persistent hope that there would be an accompanying article, but the photograph appeared to be a stand-alone item.

Meredith gave voice to her feelings. "Well, shucks. I was hoping there might be more information. I'm dying to know who these children are!" She spread her hands. "But I guess the good news is now we know that the photo was probably taken right here in Effingham County."

"Let's print out another copy of it with the date and newspaper banner on it," Julia said. "That way, at least we can show Miss Cora where it appeared in print."

"Good idea." Meredith said.

Julia looked around for a library staffer to help them. There was a small sign above a desk in one corner that said, GENEALOGICAL RESEARCH, and a tiny, wizened woman in a neat navy suit stood behind it.

"Excuse me," Julia said as she approached the woman. As she drew near, she realized there was a small name tag that said VOLUNTEER, pinned to the lady's shoulder.

"Hello, dear. How may I help you?"

"I'd like to get a copy of an article printed out from the microfilm I'm viewing. Can you tell me how to do that?"

"Certainly, dear. I'll take care of it for you. Is it an obituary?"

"Actually, it's not," Julia said. "It's a photograph."

The little woman came from behind a swinging gate and tottered over to the microfilm machine, where Meredith still stood, and peered at the screen. "Oh my," she said. "I remember my mama talking about this picture. I, of course, was still just a tot when this happened. I was born in 1932, but I can tell you this photograph caused quite a stir in its day. People talked about it for years, which is why I recall it."

"Did they?" Meredith asked. "Do you mean because the mother was offering her children for sale?"

The little woman nodded. "People were plumb scandalized that anyone would try to sell those dear babies, and a lot of folks wondered what ever had happened to them. Can you imagine?"

Both partners shook their heads. "It's hard to fathom," Julia agreed. "Do you remember anything else about the photo? Anything at all? We were wondering exactly where in Effingham this was."

The older woman hesitated. "I don't believe I ever knew. But I feel certain they were all adopted together into a good home."

"Someone mentioned that?"

Again, she hesitated. "I'm sorry, I just can't recall. It was a long, long time ago, and I only ever heard people talking about it years after the fact, you know?"

After thanking the woman for her input, Meredith and Julia headed back to the car. Julia could tell that Meredith was feeling as deflated as she was herself. They'd gleaned very little new information.

Driving back into Savannah, Meredith said, "It makes no sense. Why would Miss Cora's mother have a picture of these five children in her Bible?"

"Especially five that appear to have no connection to her," Julia added. "It would make a lot more sense if Miss Cora is the next-to-youngest child in that picture. That child would be right about her age now."

"I really wish we'd been able to learn those children's names." Meredith frowned. "What do you think we ought to do next?"

"I'm not sure." Julia felt frustrated, even though they'd found the source of the old photograph. "Miss Cora wanted us to be circumspect about this. Let's think about it and brainstorm before we proceed."

"It's a relief to hear that they were all adopted together," Meredith said.

Julia looked across the car at her friend. "If it's true. I'm not sure we can take one elderly lady's secondhand recollection as fact."

The partners were silent as they each mulled over what they had learned—or hadn't learned—from the original article.

Then another topic floated into Julia's mind. "Are you going to ride with us to the Penny's Place fundraiser?"

Meredith nodded. "I spoke to Quin, and he thought it would be fun for us all to go together."

Meredith hadn't gone last year, or the year before, Julia knew, because of Ron's death and then her own heart attack.

"Shall we let the men decide who's driving?"

Meredith nodded. "Sounds good to me."

Back at the office, Carmen was dusting when they returned. She wielded a microfiber cloth with ruthless efficiency, frowning as if the fate of the world depended on the work. The partners employed a cleaning service to vacuum and empty trash each evening and to thoroughly clean the entire first floor on weekends, but Carmen often did a little extra cleaning during the week. Heaven forbid a window or mirror should not be spotless, or a speck of dust dare to settle on one of the lovely antiques they'd chosen. Today, however, she looked unusually grim. Thinking back to the morning, Julia realized the mood had been there since their receptionist had arrived.

"You doing okay?" Julia asked as she made for the coffeepot.

Carmen sighed deeply. "I'm fine."

Julia suddenly remembered her young friend's problem from the weekend before. "Were you able to get your dryer fixed?"

Carmen shook her head. "No. I had a guy check it out yesterday. He says it's totally fried and I need a new one."

"Ugh. I know that's not in your budget," Julia said.

Carmen smiled grimly. "It is now."

Julia hesitated. Her instincts were to reassure Carmen, to offer to try to help, but she knew the young woman's pride would be offended, so she bit her tongue.

That afternoon, the partners set up their surveillance schedule for the rest of the week. Switching off was important, so the same person wasn't observed watching in the same locations every time. And Julia sometime switched vehicles with Beau so she wasn't always driving her own car.

Much as she wished she could avoid dealing with the Strieter case, she knew it wasn't workable to expect Meredith to do it all. So on Thursday, she took her turn sitting in the parking lot at

Memorial, the big medical center on Water Street, watching the big BMW. They had definitively ID'd it by the license plate, but so far neither of them had seen Oren Vance, Gaye's son-in-law.

From their research, they'd learned that Oren was an anesthesiologist at the hospital. He and Gaye's daughter had twin sons in elementary school and a toddler daughter. Three kids and a high-pressure job... Julia wouldn't be entirely surprised if indeed the man had strayed.

Just then, a dark-haired man with broad shoulders and a square jaw strode across the crosswalk from the edge of the building. He continued her way. Julia slouched down in the seat. He was wearing high-end aviator sunglasses and light blue scrubs with sneakers, and he carried a battered leather messenger bag over his shoulder. He strongly resembled the photo and description they'd acquired of Oren Vance.

He walked directly to the black BMW and slid into the driver's seat, and she could see him clipping on his seat belt before starting the car and heading out of the lot. He came out the front exit of the hospital and took the single lane that was a right-only turn onto Water Street, as Julia slowly followed, letting a car get between them. They crept up Water in a stream of heading-home traffic, and Oren turned left onto Washington Street. Two other cars were between them now, and one of them turned also, which suited Julia perfectly. Oren passed the stately First Presbyterian Church and turned right into Chatham Crescent, and at that point, Julia kept going straight. The man was going home, unless she missed her guess, and she would be much too conspicuous if she followed him bumper to bumper. Quickly, she went a block farther and turned right on

Battey. When she reached the Guckenheimer Park circle, she turned right again and immediately turned onto the Crescent coming the other way.

Oren Vance had parked in the driveway of his spacious solid brick home and was just mounting the steps of the front porch. He never even looked back as she passed, and by the time she could see him in her rearview mirror, he was closing the wide, paneled wood front door behind him.

Well. He'd gone straight home. She wondered if he could be carrying on an affair with a coworker at the hospital. But if so, he must be fairly discreet, since Gaye hadn't given them any concrete information. Perhaps Carmen or Meredith could have a word with Gaye and ask her if she had anything more solid to share about her suspicions of her son-in-law's infidelity. It would help if they knew more about his routines and any potential love interests he might have.

***

Late on Friday morning, everyone was in the office when the front door opened and Julia heard Carmen say, "Well, good morning. How are you today?"

"I'm fine, thank you, honey." The speaker was Maggie Lu. "Are you keeping these two on schedule?"

Carmen laughed. "I try."

Julia stopped perusing the file she'd been studying and rose, heading out of her office. "Maggie Lu! Hello. How nice to see you."

Maggie Lu, whom they'd met shortly after opening the agency, turned and sent Julia a brilliant smile. "Hello there. Pinky and I took a walk around Forsyth so I thought I'd stop in and say hello." She turned to a shorter woman standing behind her. "Pinky, this is my friend Julia Foley. Julia, Pinky Deveaux. We go to church together." To Julia, she said, "Pinky and I used to teach at the same school."

Julia extended her hand. "Hi, Pinky. It's a pleasure to meet you."

"You too." Pinky's handshake was firm, and her brown eyes twinkled warmly. Her skin was chestnut brown and her teeth flashed white, matching the white knitted cap she wore over her hair.

Meredith emerged from her office behind them, and the introductions were repeated. "Come on in and sit for a minute," she said, ushering the older ladies into her office and indicating the seating arrangement before the fireplace.

"We really just stopped to say hello," Maggie Lu said. "I don't want to keep you from anything."

"We've been working all morning," Julia said. "I, for one, could use a little break. Would you like some coffee?"

"That would be lovely," Maggie Lu said.

Carmen, with her sixth sense and keen hearing, was already assembling fresh coffee and a plate of fresh ganache-filled macarons from Marché de Macarons on Abercorn near the river. She bustled into the room as the women settled into their seats and began to chat.

"How's Clarissa doing?" Meredith asked. Clarissa was the only child of Maggie Lu's daughter, Charlene, and her first baby was due very, very soon.

Maggie Lu's face lit up. "She's fine," she said, drawing out the word. "Crazy girl loves being pregnant. She doesn't even mind that Philip has to haul her out of her chair now and tie her shoes. They stopped by last week, and she rested a cup of water on top of her belly. I swear, if she hadn't been holding it, that baby would have spilled it! Just kickin' and rollin' all over the place in there."

Meredith and Julia both laughed.

"She's close, right?" Julia asked. "Isn't she due the middle of this month?"

Maggie Lu nodded. "She is. Could be any day now. I can hardly wait." She clasped her hands to her chest in delight, obviously thinking about getting her hands on her first great-grandchild.

Pinky smiled. "It sure is a special time."

"Are you a Savannah native, Pinky?" Meredith asked. "Julia and I are both homegrown."

"Although I lived in Atlanta for twenty-some years before coming back here about fifteen years ago," Julia told her.

"No ma'am," Pinky said, in answer to the question. "I'm originally from Effingham, but I used to come to church with my cousins in Savannah. I met my husband there. He's from Savannah." Her cadence was soft and distinctly Southern.

At the mention of Effingham County, Meredith raised her eyebrows. "Hey, we're working on a case now that involves Effingham County history. Can I show you something?"

Pinky looked mystified but interested. "Sure."

Meredith walked to her desk and picked up a copy of the photograph from the *Effingham Herald*. "This was published in the *Herald* in 1935, and we're trying to figure out who these children are."

Pinky accepted the piece of paper and studied the images. Her face sobered as she realized what she held. "That's sad," she said, but she shook her head. "I don't recall ever hearing anything about it, though, if that's what you're asking."

Maggie Lu extended her hand, and Pinky passed her the copy. Almost instantly, Maggie Lu began nodding her head. "Oh, I've seen this before. Pinky, they reran this in the *SMN* years ago. Don't you remember?"

Pinky looked blank. "You certain? I don't recall that a'tall."

But Maggie Lu was still nodding. "Yes ma'am, I am. It was probably twenty or so years ago. There was an interview with one of the siblings, and he said he'd found some of them, but one was still missing, and they were hoping to find the last one. Folks wrote in and said it must be a hoax, that nobody would sell their own children, but he stuck by his story. I don't recall if he ever found the last one though."

"I don't remember that either," Meredith said, clearly vexed with herself.

"Maggie Lu, that's fantastic!" Julia was elated. "We've been looking for this information. You say it was twenty years ago, give or take?"

Their friend's mouth pursed as she narrowed her eyes in thought. "Maybe thirty," she admitted. "I forget how old I am sometimes."

"Don't we all?" Meredith asked wryly, and they all chuckled. Meredith leaned forward. "If you could narrow down the time frame at all, it would help us enormously."

"You don't want much," Maggie Lu remarked, making Meredith laugh again. She sat back, taking a sip of her coffee as the others fell silent. "Now let's see," she said. "It was after Jacob died." Jacob was Maggie Lu's elder child and only son, and Julia knew he'd died during Operation Desert Storm in 1991.

The others fell silent.

Finally, Pinky said softly, "You sure about that?"

Maggie Lu nodded, looking down into her coffee cup. "I know I had lost one of my babies when I read that," she murmured. "It struck a nerve, that anyone could sell their kids."

Meredith reached over and laid her hand atop Maggie Lu's. "I can imagine it did."

Everyone was silent for a moment.

"So that would have been a bit less than thirty years ago," Maggie Lu finally said. "And it was summer."

"Summer?" Pinky looked surprised. "Now why on earth would you remember that?"

"I remember," Maggie Lu said firmly. "It was boilin' hot, and all I could think about was how hot that little cabin must have been back then." She gazed into the distance again but finally shook her head. "Can't remember anything more specific."

"You know what you ought to do?" Pinky asked. "You ought to take that picture to a nursing home. Those folks might remember more about it, since they'd have been livin' and workin' here during the time that was published."

"That's a grand idea, Pinky," Meredith said. She turned to Maggie Lu. "Thanks for bringing her along today."

Maggie Lu smiled. "My pleasure." Then she said, "I'm going to visit Delyse at Rutgers tomorrow. I could take a copy of that along and ask some of the other residents. Delyse probably won't know, but there's a fellow named Baruch Helms who might." Delyse was a friend and former volunteer at the Henry Street library where Maggie Lu volunteered, but she'd developed Alzheimer's Disease three years ago and had recently been admitted to a local nursing home.

"Baruch Helms." Pinky breathed the name as if it was a prayer. "Oh yes, Baruch might be able to help." She looked at Julia and Meredith. "Baruch is odd. I had him in school when he was little. I was young then, and he was such a puzzle. He can remember the dates of everything that happens around him, and he never forgets your name if he's met you just once. I know he can read because he reads the paper every day, but he can't do figures. He can't make change or anything. He'd work all day and be happy with a dime." She rolled her eyes. "His mama used to get so mad at people who took advantage of him."

"His mama died last year," Maggie Lu added, "and Baruch's in the home now because he can't take care of himself and he doesn't have any other family." She nodded. "If Baruch ever read about that photo, I'm guessing he'll remember the date he saw it."

Julia felt a shiver of excitement raise goose bumps on her arms. "He could be an incredible resource. I can't imagine how we'll ever find it otherwise. Could we go along?"

"Sure. You both can. I'll call you in the morning," Maggie Lu said.

"Oh, I can't." Meredith couldn't hide her disappointment. "Carter's family is going to be in town again, so Carmen and I are taking Kaden, Kinsley, and Harmony—Carmen's little friend from the Boys & Girls Club—ice-skating at the Civic Center tomorrow morning." The Civic Center had been transformed into an ice arena open to the public for three weeks in December. "I have no intention of getting on the ice," Meredith said, chuckling, "but we thought the kids would enjoy it." She turned to Julia. "But you go along with them. We need to find out more about that picture."

"So I'll let you know what time to meet us," Maggie Lu said to Julia. She set her coffee cup down. "We've taken up enough of your day, and we've not finished our walk yet. Come on, Pinky, let's get back to it."

Pinky smiled and rose to her feet. "It was nice to meet you both."

"You too," Julia said as Meredith murmured a farewell. "Thanks for your help with our little project."

Meredith hurried over to the office to make a copy of the article, and the two older ladies departed.

Julia watched them walk down the steps, cross Whitaker Street, and stroll along one of the shaded sidewalks that curved in patterns through the park. "Crossing my fingers," she said to Meredith, holding up her pointer and middle fingers to show her friend. "It would be a complete miracle if this Baruch fellow recalls when that was in the paper."

Chapter Five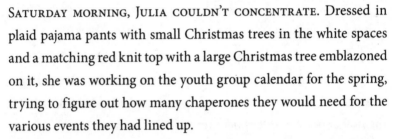

Saturday morning, Julia couldn't concentrate. Dressed in plaid pajama pants with small Christmas trees in the white spaces and a matching red knit top with a large Christmas tree emblazoned on it, she was working on the youth group calendar for the spring, trying to figure out how many chaperones they would need for the various events they had lined up.

She looked at the schedule again. For the progressive dinner, they needed nine homes, because the youth group was so large they split the kids into three more manageable groups for the event. Three homes for each course: hors d'oerves, a salad, and the main course and vegetables. For dessert, they would gather back at the church and toast s'mores around the fire pit at the back of the building.

They also needed drivers. Twenty-seven teens had signed up for the late January event. If they sent nine kids to each of the three houses, they'd need two to three drivers per house, depending on how big the drivers' vehicles were. Julia herself could carry four passengers in her car. She scribbled some notes on the piece of paper before her.

As she wondered for the tenth time what time Maggie Lu would be going to the nursing home, her cell phone rang. She snatched it up, seeing Maggie Lu's name on the caller ID. "Hey there."

Maggie Lu chuckled. "Hey, yourself. How's eleven o'clock work?"

"Eleven's fine," Julia said. It was barely ten now. "See you then." Ending the call, Julia scrambled out of her seat at the breakfast nook, leaving her youth group plans spread across the table, and rushed upstairs to shower and change.

She blew her silver hair dry with a round brush to give it a bit of style, all the effort she usually put into it, and dressed in beige slacks with a navy twinset striped in beige as well. She slipped into comfortable navy ballet flats, grabbed her purse, and made the drive to Rutgers Nursing Home. Maggie Lu had helped to place Delyse at Rutgers when Alzheimer's made it impossible for the old woman to live at home anymore.

A few minutes before eleven, she parked before the comfortable, sprawling facility and approached the visitors' entrance in the central building, which was flanked by long wings. Two large evergreens in front of the building were covered with lights, and although they didn't show up well during the day, Julia imagined that at night they were a striking sight.

She was buzzed in after she hit a button and gave her name. The front door unlocked, and when she entered, she was greeted by a receptionist who gave her a visitor's badge after she signed the guest register. She stood for a moment, looking around a pleasant lobby with wing chairs and love seats in two groupings flanking a pretty white stone fireplace. A handsome fern stood atop a buffet along a far wall. A large Christmas tree with colored lights and large shiny silver ornaments matched a large blue-and-silver-bedecked wreath above the fireplace, and other Christmas decor in the same color theme was placed on the occasional tables around the room.

Above the fern, several portraits of famous scientists and inventors made a pleasing display. Julia walked over to read the plaques underneath. George Washington Carver, agricultural inventor; Mae C. Jemison, the first black female astronaut; Otis Boykin, whose twenty-six patents included a control unit for the pacemaker—

"Good morning, Julia." Turning, she saw Maggie Lu and Pinky approaching. Pneumatic double doors that led to the interior of the building closed behind them, and Julia heard the snick of a lock.

"Morning," she replied. "Nice security here."

Maggie Lu smiled and nodded. "It's one of many things I like about it. The patients are closely monitored, and it would be very difficult for someone to escape. Many dementia sufferers wander off, so it was important to me to have Delyse in a safe, caring setting where that couldn't happen."

"We've been with her all morning," Pinky said.

"Oh. I could have come earlier," Julia said, chagrinned.

"No, no, I waited to call you until we knew when we'd be done visiting," Maggie Lu said. "She can get a little agitated with strangers now, and I don't believe she would remember you. We fed her breakfast and took her to get her hair done, and then we just caught her up on church doings and sang some hymns and things with her."

"That sounds like a labor of love," Julia said. "How's she doing?"

Maggie Lu shook her head. "Declining, as we've been told to expect." She paused, her chin quivering. "It's hard to see a dear friend go through this."

Julia put a comforting arm around her friend. "I'm sure it is."

Maggie Lu took a deep breath. "But you're here to meet Baruch today. Oh, I hope he can help you."

"He's down this wing," Pinky said, indicating a set of the locked double doors that led to a wing on the right.

Maggie Lu punched in a code, and the doors unlocked so the women could enter. Maggie Lu and Pinky led her down a hallway that divided into three sections. Every resident's door was decorated with a Christmas stocking that had been personalized with his or her name. The women turned left, and after passing several rooms, paused at a nurses' station where a nurse in a Santa-themed scrub top with red and silver strips woven into her cornrows looked up and smiled.

"Good morning," Maggie Lu said to her. "We're here to visit Baruch Helms."

"Oh, he'll love that. He doesn't get many visitors, and he's one of the few here who can really interact with and appreciate you." The woman pointed down the hallway. "I believe he's still in the breakfast room. He likes to help clean up."

The three women proceeded down the hallway to a large, bright room at the end. Chairs and tables were grouped around the room, and spider plants, ivy, and golden pothos hung in the windows. A pair of grizzled old men sat at a table by one window with a chess match in progress between them.

Christmas was everywhere in this room too, Julia saw. A big tree stood in front of the center window. There were white lights and shiny red balls all over it and all the ornaments appeared to have been homemade by the residents, many likely with help. Each of the dining tables had a centerpiece of holly, red Christmas balls and white-sprayed pinecones, and oversized ornaments made of unbreakable acrylic hung on ribbon from the joints of the ceiling tiles.

Another man was scurrying around picking up salt and pepper shakers and placing them in a basket. He was of medium height, so slender his black pants were belted to the last notch, and with them he wore sneakers and a long-sleeved T-shirt with a smiling elf on the front neatly tucked in. He had a frizzy halo of close-cropped hair. The moment he saw them enter, he set his basket down and came rushing over.

"Good morning! Breakfast over. You want a sandwich? I talk to the cook. Breakfast over," he repeated.

Maggie Lu smiled. "Hi, Baruch. Do you remember me? Miss Maggie Lu from church?"

Baruch nodded. "Miss Maggie Lu. You took care of Miss Delyse till she got sick and come here. My mama died, so I be here too. You came to Mama's funeral. November 7, 2019."

Maggie Lu nodded gently. "Yes, honey. I did. And here's Mrs. Deveaux. You remember her?"

"Miz Deveaux my teacher," Baruch said. "Used to wear a pretty blue dress. I liked that dress." He looked at Pinky. "You still wear the blue dress?"

Pinky grinned. "I don't fit into that blue dress anymore, Baruch. Sure wish I did."

"You know Santa's coming, right? Santa's going to bring me presents!"

"I bet he is. What you want for Christmas, Baruch?"

"Mama always gave me a new pair of pants and new shirts." He looked down at his clothes, fingering a ragged patch at one pocket. "Need some new clothes."

"I'll make sure Santa knows that." Maggie Lu looked meaningfully at Pinky. Then she drew Julia forward. "Baruch, this is our friend Mrs. Foley. She has a question she'd like to ask you about the newspaper."

"The *Savannah Morning News*. 'Light of the Coastal Empire and Lowcountry.' Savannah-Now-dot-com." He spouted the paper's motto and online URL. "I read the paper every morning," Baruch said. "Hi, Mrs. Foley. You in the paper sometimes. You a judge."

"Yes, I was," Julia said, stunned that he would recognize her. "I'm retired now."

"May 27, 2018," Baruch said.

Julia's mouth fell open. "That's correct! I retired on May 27, 2018!"

Baruch nodded. "In the paper on Wednesday, May 30."

Julia clapped her hands. "Wow. It was announced a few days later." She turned to Maggie Lu. "I'm not sure I could have told you when, though." Her hopes rose. How would this man—this child in a man's body—know that? She remembered what Pinky said about his unusual recall. It really must be true. *Please,* she thought, *let him remember the rerun of the 1935 photograph.*

Pinky said, "Baruch, Mrs. Foley is going to ask you about something else in the paper. If you can remember anything, you tell her, all right?"

Baruch nodded solemnly. "I'll remember." Then he grinned, a huge toothy smile that Julia couldn't resist, and she smiled in return. "I'm a good remember-er," he said.

Julia crossed her fingers. She hoped he was right. "Baruch, I'm trying to find out when a photograph was published. The picture was about five children who were sold. There might have been an article with it." She pulled the copy of the old photo from her bag and held it out. "Do you remember that at all?"

"August 22, 1992," Baruch said after taking a glance at the picture. "Page 5. August 22 was a Saturday."

"What?" Julia scrambled to yank a notepad and pen from her purse. "Saturday, August 22 of 1992. Are you sure?"

Pinky laughed. "We told you what Baruch can do."

"I'm sure," Baruch said, as if he'd had to reassure people thousands of times. Which he probably had. "Page five."

"He's like a living file folder," Maggie Lu explained. "I don't doubt him for a minute."

"Oh, wow. Baruch, I can't thank you enough. This is huge! I've got to get over to the library." Julia glanced at her watch. "They're open until two on Saturday. I might be able to get that article today."

"You want a sandwich? Breakfast over," Baruch reminded her again.

"Not today, thank you," Julia told him. "I have to go, but I really appreciate your help. Merry Christmas, Baruch. I'm sure Santa will be by to visit you."

Minutes later, the three women were back in the front lobby.

"Is there anything I can do for him?" Julia asked the two older women. "Could I pay him for helping me?"

Maggie Lu shook her head. "He doesn't handle money."

"But," said Pinky, "you could make a little donation to his care if you like. Our church keeps an account in his name, against the day his mama's money runs out."

"That's a wonderful idea," Julia said. "I'll do that." She dug in her purse and came up with three twenties. "But listen, this isn't for his care, exactly. Will you buy him a Christmas gift for me? Pants, a shirt, whatever you think he'd like? I'd do it, but I don't know his sizes or if there's a certain brand he usually wears."

Maggie Lu smiled. "We can do that. Santa Claus thanks you."

"Santa Claus wishes she could see his face when he opens them," Julia said with a grin. She gave each woman a kiss on the cheek. "Thank you, thank you, thank you! Talk to you later."

"Let us know how your search goes," Maggie Lu called after her. "This is the most excitement we've had in weeks!"

Julia shot them a thumbs-up, grinning as the receptionist hit the button at the desk to unlock the front door so she could leave.

She drove back into town and headed straight to the Bull Street Library. It was noon now. With any luck, she could locate that article today. She found a spot in the lot, which was a minor miracle—in keeping with the day so far, she decided as she hopped out of her car and hurried up the side steps.

The Georgia Room was busy, probably because it was Saturday. She had to wait a long ten minutes until she could take a seat in front of a microfilm machine with the prized reel containing the date in question.

Finally, a woman with faded red hair gave up her seat with a friendly smile. "Who are you looking for?" she asked.

"I beg your pardon?" Julia wasn't sure what the woman meant.

"Surnames," the woman said patiently. She gestured around the room. "Seems like almost everyone who has come in here this morning is doing genealogical research. I'm visiting from Mobile, and I'm taking the opportunity to look up some ancestors that started out here in Savannah."

"Oh, I see." Julia smiled. "Welcome to Savannah. I'm actually not doing genealogical research, just looking up a reprint of an article."

The woman nodded. "Well, there goes my hope that maybe I'm meeting a distant cousin who's also searching for common ancestors."

Julia laughed. "Sorry to burst your bubble."

The woman took her leave, and Julia quickly set up the microfilm and began to scroll through the year until she reached late summer. August 20, August 21...there it was. August 22, 1992. She could feel her heart beating faster. Maggie Lu had been so certain Baruch was right. What if he wasn't? They'd be right back to square one. Still, she reassured herself, she'd seen evidence of his memory firsthand. He'd known the date she retired. The actual date! Surely he was as accurate about this as he had been about that.

Her eyes flickered over the pages until she reached page five. And there, just below the fold, was the very image she had in her purse. Only this time, there was an article below it.

Depression Mystery, read the title.

Five children from rural Guyton, GA, were offered for sale in this July 14, 1935, photo. One of those children, Sumner Denton, 65, has come forward to share his story, in hopes that a final missing sibling can be found. Sold at age seven as household help to a Guyton widow, Denton was able to track down two of his siblings who were sold together for farm work. A third sibling was adopted but later died of pneumonia. The fourth sibling is believed to have been adopted, but Denton has never been able to discover her whereabouts.

Denton's father, Mason, was killed in a farming accident shortly before his fifth child's birth. His wife, Mildred, was unable to keep the family together. She died less than a year after the children were sold. Records indicate she drowned in a farm pond, and Denton believes she committed suicide.

Denton's missing sister was born around 1932 and might be 60 years old this year. Denton does not know her full given name or her date of birth. In the black-and-white photograph, she appears to be a toddler with blond hair and light eyes, possibly blue. She would have been two or three years old at the time of her adoption. Anyone with information about the child should contact Phil Marven at the Savannah Morning News. *"I don't know what happened to her, but I'll search for her until I take my last breath," says Sumner.*

Sumner Denton! She repeated the name several times in her mind, thrilled to have found one of the children's names. The reporter's name wasn't familiar to Julia, but she knew exactly who to call. One of her newspaper contacts from her juvenile court years might be able to tell her how to find Phil Marven. Maybe he could tell her if Sumner had found his siblings.

She printed out a copy of the article and shot Meredith a quick text to let her know she'd found it. She'd tell her the rest in person, and then they could find contact information for Sumner Denton and speak with him...if he was still living and still of sound mind. She thought of Maggie Lu's friend Delyse. The man would be in his early nineties now, she realized, and very easily could be unable to tell her much of anything. Her euphoria faded a little. Before trying to speak with him, she really wanted to talk to the reporter who'd done the rerun of the photo and who'd interviewed Sumner, the eldest child.

She scrolled through her phone contacts until she found Harper Finch's phone number. Harper had been a classmate of Meredith's older son Carter and had been working for the *SMN* for almost two decades now.

"Hello, Julia," Harper answered her cell phone on the third ring. "Merry-almost-Christmas."

"The same to you, Harper," Julia responded. "Do you have a minute?"

"Always, if it involves a possible story," Harper declared. "What's up?"

"Do you know how I can contact Phil Marven? He used to work at the paper in 1992. Is he still there?"

"Aw, Julia." Regret replaced the lilt in Harper's voice. "Phil died of pancreatic cancer. Let's see, I believe that was 2010. Why did you want to talk to him?"

Julia exhaled heavily, deeply disappointed by the news. "I wanted to talk with him about a story he ran in 1992. Five kids from Guyton who were put up for sale in 1935. Does that ring a bell? The eldest child was trying to find one of the siblings he'd never been able to locate. I wondered if he'd ever found her, and I thought Phil might have contact information for him."

Harper's voice still sounded lazy and relaxed, but Julia could almost sense her keen interest over the connection. "You investigating for someone?"

"We're just curious about it," Julia prevaricated.

"Phil's widow gave us his files after he died," Harper said, "and most of his stuff was digital and easily added to our system. Let me check and see what I can find." She cleared her throat. "In exchange for you being straight with me if you uncover a story, all right?"

Julia shook her head before realizing that Harper couldn't see her. "I'm really just hoping to speak with the man who was interviewed. Now that I know his name, I should be able to locate him."

"Is one of the other children your client?" Harper asked.

"No," Julia answered truthfully. "I don't even know if any of the children are still alive, to be honest. But if I find out they are, I'll let you know."

Harper sighed. "I know you're not telling me everything. But I'll look back and see what I can find."

"Thanks, Harper," Julia said. "I really appreciate it."

She checked her watch. It was after lunchtime now. Beau wouldn't be home from the golf course yet, so she still had some time. She texted Meredith. YOU BACK FROM THE SKATING EXPEDITION? I HAVE NEWS.

Meredith replied almost instantly. HOME NOW. YOU IN TOWN? STOP BY.

WILL YOU FEED ME?

Meredith's reply was a laugh emoji. SURE THING.

Julia headed back to the parking lot and got back onto Bull Street heading north. At Gordon Street, she turned right and when she reached Habersham Street, she went north again until she reached Meredith's home on Troup Square. She pulled into the alley behind the house and parked in Meredith's drive, then let herself into the gate and headed up the back steps to the main floor of the house.

"Yoo-hoo," she called as she opened the door that led into a minuscule mudroom.

"Hey, come on in." Meredith popped her head around the corner from the kitchen. "We had pulled pork for lunch. I'm making you a sandwich now."

"That sounds heavenly," Julia said.

"And some leftover cornbread and a salad," Meredith added, disappearing from view.

Before entering the kitchen, Julia peeked through the cased doorway into the formal living room. "Oh, your tree is gorgeous."

"Thank you," Meredith said. "I do the same thing every year, so it's no surprise."

"I still love it." Julia took a moment to admire all the ornaments amid the white lights, and the iridescent garland that made the tree sparkle so. Interspersed with them were a huge number of antique ornaments: teardrops, lanterns, Santa faces, fruits, snowmen, pinecones, and many fancifully shaped balls with radiant stars and other designs in them.

"I bet you have the biggest collection of antique ornaments in town," she called.

"Maybe," came the answer. It sounded like Meredith was grinning.

"You should put your house on the Home Tour some year," Julia said.

"Are you nuts?"

Julia laughed as she entered the light sage kitchen with its painted cabinets, light maple butcher block island, and gleaming stainless appliances, and asked, "Where is everyone?"

"The kids are watching a movie upstairs while their parents walk down to the river. Apparently ice-skating is exhausting." Meredith grinned, assembling a wicker tray on the island with Julia's meal and a glass of sweet tea. "Let's go sit on the deck. It's too cool to be buggy today." She suited action to words, picking up the tray and walking through the white-framed French doors onto the deck. It was pleasant in the midday sun, and a mild breeze wound around them.

Another Christmas tree stood on the deck. Unlike the artificial one in the living room, this was a live tree in a bucket. It also was festooned with white lights, but the only other decor was big silver balls and silver bows firmly tied here and there to resist wind. A larger silver bow trailed long ribbons down the sides of the tree.

Meredith set the tray down on a central coffee table and sank into the cushions of a solid wing chair in espresso seagrass wicker. "Now tell me what you found out. Did that fella Maggie Lu mentioned really remember the article?" She sounded skeptical.

Julia took a seat in a matching chair nearby, accepting the plate containing her sandwich. "Yum. Thank you so much." She took a deep breath. "You are not going to believe this. Not only did Baruch remember the date, but he told me which page of the paper it was on." She produced the copy of the reprinted photo and article with a flourish. "Voilà!"

"Oh my goodness. You're right. I can't believe it. How is that possible?" It was a rhetorical question.

As Julia tucked into her sandwich, Meredith took the offered paper and read the brief article. Julia watched her, enjoying the tasty lunch.

Finally, Meredith looked up. "I do believe Miss Cora *thinks* she's an only child, but I have to wonder if her parents adopted her and just never told her."

"I know." Julia suspected the same thing. They both fell silent for a moment. The implications of what they suspected could be enormous.

"Have you ever heard anything about Miss Cora being adopted?" Meredith asked. "Because I sure haven't."

Julia shook her head, although Meredith, with her socially high-powered background and lifelong connections in Savannah, was more likely to have heard any hints of such a thing than she.

The partners stared at each other.

"It could be purely coincidental," Meredith said hopefully.

"It could." Julia nodded, although she could see that Meredith was having as hard a time believing that as she was. "But we can't say anything. We especially can't mention it to Harper Finch."

"Harper Finch? What's she got to do with this?" Meredith asked.

Julia realized she had left out some very important details. "I called Harper to see if she could put me in touch with Phil Marven, the reporter who wrote that 1992 story. But he passed away, and Harper offered to go through his research files and see if she could find out if he learned anything more."

Meredith was silent for a moment. Finally, she said, "That's a problem. Harper's going to want to know what we know and why we're looking into this."

"I told her we were just interested," Julia said. She related the conversation about Sumner Denton, the eldest brother. "I didn't lie," she said. "We're not investigating for him. And we don't know if he or any of the others are even still living. I guess that's the next thing we need to try to find out."

Meredith shook her head. "This is getting sticky. We absolutely cannot divulge anything about Miss Cora."

"No," Julia agreed instantly. "We can't."

The Interview, Part 2

Interview with my great-grandfather Sumner Denton, age 93, Guyton, GA 10/12/2020.

Interviewer: *So, you were sold first, and you didn't know what happened to your four younger brothers and sisters. Did you ever find out anything about them?*

SD: Just one brother. The other three were all sisters. Burdie and I sure were disappointed when that last baby popped out and we were told she was a girl. Yeah, eventually I learned about the others. Mrs. Healy, my lady, lived right in Guyton. In the town, I mean. I helped her with housework, and I chopped wood for the winter, and I took care of the horse and the old milk cow she had. Got cussed out when she found out I didn't know how to milk. A couple of months or so, I guess it was, after I got sold, Mrs. Healy up and out of the blue one day, says, "I know where your brother and the oldest girl are livin.'" I must have just looked at her like a fool, because she said it again. And then she said, "They look like they ain't been fed real good." So, after she told me where they were, I sneaked over one Sunday to see if I could see Burdie and Bobbie Dee. They got bought by a farmer who lived outside of town, and they worked hard, though I figure they weren't even old enough for school when they first went there. He had them out weeding his garden and shooing flies away from the cattle so they didn't get warbles, shucking peas, picking tobacco—stuff little kids shouldn't have been doing day and night. Mrs. Healy always gave me Sundays off after church except for morning and evening chores, and that day she left a big loaf of bread and some cheese on the table and said, "If you're goin' on a ramble, you better take plenty of provisions." So I wrapped up that bread and cheese and took it right along with me. I reckon it was a two- or three-mile walk out of town to that farm, but I did it, and then I hid for a couple of hours and watched the house. The farmer and his wife and three kids got in their Ford Model T—it was a 1927, same year as me, which is why I always recall it—and off they went to visit relatives for Sunday dinner. A little while after they left, I saw two kids come out of this little shed off the kitchen. I figured it was the wash-shed, and as it turned out I was right. But it also was where my brother and sister slept, except for the few days in the winter when it was really cold, and then they got to sleep by the woodstove. Those two kids were Burdie and Bobbie Dee, and boy, were they glad to see me. They ate that bread and cheese up like they were starved, and I guess they weren't far from it, because they sure were puny. So, after that, I sneaked over there near every Sunday with food Mrs. Healy set out for me. Those two had it rough, that's for sure.

Interviewer: *What about your two youngest sisters? Did you ever find them?*

SD: Corie was the next to youngest, and I never heard a single other thing about her when I was growing up. She just disappeared. See, I didn't know their names. Their real names, I mean. My brother's name was Burdie, spelled B-u-r-d-i-e, for Burdett, but for years, I thought it was like a bird. And my sisters were Bobbie Dee, Corie, and Tillie. They were all nicknames, see? So, I didn't even know my siblings' real names. It was just luck and Mrs. Healy that found Tillie.

Interviewer: *Tillie was the baby?*

SD: Yes. She wasn't even walking when we got sold. Mrs. Healy, she just listened for gossip everywhere she went, and soon she heard at our church that a baby popped up out of nowhere to a couple that came there. Folks said the lady never was pregnant, and a couple of them said she bought one of those babies from the poor woman who killed herself....

Interviewer: *And...?*

SD: Mrs. Healy, she heard that baby's name was Matilda, so I figured it wasn't Tillie. But as it turns out, Tillie's a nickname for Matilda, so it was my baby sister. I got to see her sometimes at church with her mama and daddy, but she didn't know me. Their house was a nice place, and I reckon

Tillie probably was happy and forgot all about us, being so young and all. But then she got pneumonia when she was about eight years old. And she died.

Interviewer: *Your baby sister Tillie died?*

SD: Yes. They said she wasn't sick real long. She was just too little.... So that's how I lost both my littlest sisters.

Chapter Six

JULIA WAS DOZING ON SUNDAY morning, enjoying a rare opportunity to laze in bed for an extra hour. Beau had gotten up at six thirty to hit the treadmill, and she was just lying there, debating. Should she make French toast or Southwestern omelets for breakfast? Should she wear the red sweater set with black slacks or the forest green dress to church? Suddenly, the buzzing of her cell phone on the bedside table interrupted her contemplation. She rolled over to reach for the phone, pulling the blankets around her in a cocoon. Ugh. It was only six forty-five. Who could that be? She had to grab her reading glasses to see the message on the screen. It was from Meredith.

HARPER MUST NEED A STORY BAD. OUR PHOTO IS IN TODAY'S PAPER!

Julia sat bolt upright, flinging back the covers. Furiously, she texted back.

OH NO! WE'VE GOT TO WARN MISS CORA. I DON'T WANT HER SEEING THAT OVER BREAKFAST. She added an emoji that looked wide-eyed and horrified to get her point across, then typed, I'LL CALL HER AT 7.

Why on earth would Harper have rerun that article again? Agitated, she padded through the house to the coffeepot and poured herself a large cup of fresh coffee from the pot Beau had made. Then she settled onto a stool at the island and scanned SavannahNow. com, the online version of the paper. She quickly found Harper's rewrite. It was mostly the original information and didn't include anything Julia didn't already know. Magnolia Investigations was the new contact.

They must have had to pull something, she thought absently. Maybe an ad that hadn't been paid for, or some other story that had lost its cachet for one reason or another. Whatever had happened, they were going to have to break the news to Miss Cora.

It was almost seven. She laid down her phone, picked it back up again, and thumbed through her contacts until she came to the entry for Cora Butler Chisholm. Miss Cora had been an only child, Julia recalled her telling them. But surely, if the Chisholms had suddenly appeared with a toddler out of nowhere, questions would have been asked. Someone would still remember, and people would have spoken of it since. Julia might not have been in a position to hear such gossip, but Meredith and her family certainly were, and she didn't appear to have ever heard a whisper.

Then again, Miss Cora had said they lived in Buckhead when she was a baby. Given the nature of society and secrecy almost a century ago, Julia thought it might be plausible that Cora's parents had moved away with the idea of adopting and passing off a child as their own. Stranger things had happened.

The digital display on the phone said seven. Julia hit the touch screen where Miss Cora's number was highlighted, and as it began to ring, she touched the SPEAKER button.

"Chisholm residence, Susan speaking."

"Good morning, Susan, it's Julia Foley."

"Good morning, Mrs. Foley. You're getting an early start to the Lord's day." There was a smile and a question in Susan's voice.

"I'm sorry to bother you so early, Susan," Julia said, "but if Miss Cora's awake, it's very important that I speak with her. If she's not, I need you to do me a favor and have her call me as soon as she gets up before she starts reading the paper."

"Before she starts reading the paper?" Susan sounded mystified. "Lucky for you, I just heard her moving around upstairs. Let me have her call you as soon as she comes down."

"That would be great," Julia said.

"And I'll hide the paper until you've talked," Susan added, chuckling.

"You're a treasure," Julia said. "Thank you, Susan."

It was a full fifteen minutes before her cell phone rang. By then, she was sitting out on the deck in one of the brushed steel patio chairs that swiveled, sipping coffee and idly reading through the print version of the paper that hadn't even been delivered until after she'd called Miss Cora.

"Julia Foley," she said, hitting the SPEAKER button. She'd gotten lazy since the advent of the mobile phone. She hated holding that little thing up to her ear.

"Good morning, Julia. This is Cora Chisholm. I'm sorry I missed your call."

Julia took a moment to marvel that someone as high on the Savannah social ladder as Cora Butler Chisholm would be calling and speaking so casually to her. "No, I'm sorry to have called so early," she said. "But I had some news that couldn't wait."

"Have you learned something about that picture?" Miss Cora asked.

"We have," Julia said. "It was first published in Effingham County in 1935, but it was reprinted in the *SMN* in 1992. The second time, there was an article with it about the eldest child, who was trying to find all his siblings. He'd located two and one had passed away, but there was one more he hadn't found yet. We're going to try to contact him next to see if he ever found his brother and sisters."

"But you still don't know why my mama would have kept that picture?" Miss Cora asked.

"No, ma'am, we don't." It wasn't a lie, Julia assured herself. A suspicion was definitely not a fact. "But I called you this morning because I wanted to let you know the picture was run in the paper again this morning."

"My stars!" Miss Cora sounded surprised but not dismayed. "What a coincidence!"

Julia couldn't help but smile. "Actually, that's my doing, I'm afraid. It doesn't mention you," she hastened to assure the older lady. "The reporter who wrote about it in 1992 passed away, and another reporter is looking through his files to see if he learned anything. And I guess she decided to put it out there one more time in case anything else comes to light."

"Maybe you'll learn something new," Miss Cora said hopefully. "I just can't help thinking there's more to the story that I'd like to know."

Or maybe not, Julia thought with a shiver of apprehension. "I'll certainly let you know if we learn anything else," she said. As she ended the call, she couldn't help wondering if Miss Cora would recognize the similarity between the missing sibling's age and her own.

***

Julia had high hopes that something might shake loose to give them more information. She had decided not to bug Harper on Sunday, but she had more questions for the reporter. That would be the first call of her Monday morning, she decided as she unpacked her briefcase and booted up her computer in her office. Sitting at her desk, she punched Harper's number into her office phone and hit the SPEAKER button.

"Good morning, Harper Finch with the *Savannah Morning News*. How may I help you?" Apparently, she hadn't recognized the office number.

"Good morning, Harper, it's Julia Foley."

"Morning, Julia." Harper sounded a bit tentative. "I hope you didn't mind me running the article again. I couldn't stop thinking about it, and when my boss said he needed to move some things around, I snagged the open space."

"Well, we haven't even had a chance to try to contact the brother that Phil interviewed," Julia said. "He may have found them all in the past twenty-eight years."

"I tried looking him up and couldn't get any answer," Harper said. "So I figured maybe the story would shake something loose."

"Have you had a chance to go through the old files and see if Phil learned anything after the article ran?"

Harper sighed. "The number for Sumner Denton that Phil had is not in service anymore. That's not unusual in this age of mobile phones. I searched obituaries and didn't find one, but that doesn't mean he isn't deceased. I mean, he'd be really old by now. He could be living in a nursing home, or he could have passed away and I just didn't find a record of it."

"I can try searching as well," Julia said. "Anything else come to light?"

"Precious little," Harper said. "There really wasn't much reaction at all. Certainly, no one came forward to say she was his long-lost sister."

"Okay. Thanks for letting me know," Julia said.

"You'd better keep me posted if you learn anything new," Harper said, and there was a lightness in her voice that told Julia she was grinning. "I nearly had to flatten two other reporters to get that space. Make it worth my while."

Carmen had made coffee while Julia was on the call, and Julia poured herself a generous cup before sticking her head into the reception area. "Good morning. How was your weekend?"

Carmen shrugged. "Okay. I bought a new dryer. It's being delivered and installed first thing tomorrow, so I'll need to come in a little late."

"No problem. One of us can make sure we're in the office until you arrive. Where'd you get it?"

"Stanley's Appliances," Carmen answered. "They are having some pretty good holiday sales. I really hated to do it, because now I'm going to have to push back the date I can buy a new car, and I was really hoping to have something with AC by the end of March before it starts getting too hot again." She sighed and shrugged. "Oh well, people lived without air-conditioning for thousands of years. It's really not that big a deal."

Julia didn't know how to respond. It was hard watching the young woman struggle for basic comfort that she took for granted, but she knew better than to express sympathy. "I'm glad you got your dryer," she said simply.

"What's on the agenda for today?" Carmen asked, turning the subject to business. "I saw that the paper ran Miss Cora's photo yesterday. Maybe we'll get some leads out of it."

"I hope so," Julia said. "The first thing I'm going to do is try to track down Sumner Denton, who was interviewed for the first article."

She headed back into her office and settled in front of her computer. The first place she intended to look was the Social Security Administration Death Index. The agency had registered with it upon opening as a part of their basic information search capability, and she quickly logged in and entered the limited information she had. Unfortunately, no records were returned. The database was only updated through 2014, which she didn't understand. Why wouldn't they be updated through at least the year before last? Still, she reasoned that if he'd died more recently than that, he would have shown up in a Google search. It was true that Harper had said she'd already tried that method, but there was no harm in trying again. A general internet search might well yield an obituary.

She tried that next, but like Harper before her, found nothing.

Okay, maybe Sumner Denton was still living. But where? He could still be in Georgia. He could be in South Carolina quite easily.

Or he could be farther afield. Sighing, she entered his name into the search engines to which they subscribed.

And again, she got no hits, although she did learn that there were over two thousand Dentons listed in Georgia and nearly a thousand more in South Carolina.

"Shucks," she said aloud. "That wasn't helpful at all."

Meredith, who had just entered the building from the back, paused in the doorway. "Good morning. What wasn't helpful?"

"I'm trying to track down Sumner Denton," Julia said. "He'd be pretty old if he's still living, but I can't find an obituary, so I'd have to say it's a possibility."

Meredith made a face. "That will actually make him harder to find. He could be anywhere. If he had children who moved away, he could be living somewhere else with them by now."

Julia sighed. "I know."

"He might be in a nursing home, or he might be living with a family member. Is there any way to find out if he ever married and had kids?"

Julia lifted her hands helplessly. "Not easily, especially not without knowing the names of any family members. We could check for marriage records at Effingham County Courthouse, but that's assuming he stayed in Effingham."

"And that's a big if," Meredith said.

The partners fell silent. What other ways could they use to try to track down Sumner Denton?

Julia gestured to the computer before her. "Give me a couple of minutes to make notes on what I've done, and we can work on a schedule for the week. I guess we've got some more surveillance to plan."

"Actually," Meredith said, "I did a little drive-by of the Pettis home this morning. It was a little out of my way, but I just wanted to see what was up first thing in the morning."

"Anything exciting?"

"Not much." Meredith reached into her purse. "But check this out. Hilly Pettis's front yard has three missing shrubs beneath the big front window. Looks like maybe someone's getting ready to replace them."

"What?" Julia shot out of her seat as Meredith withdrew the digital camera from the bag and turned it on. There had been several overgrown arbor vitae crammed into the space before. She hovered over her friend, poring over the images Meredith slowly scrolled through on the screen. "But we don't know who did the digging? No people in the pics?"

Meredith shook her head. "Sorry, no. It must have been done yesterday. There was no one about today, and the car the husband usually drives was already gone."

"Do those kids walk to school? I wonder if one of them drives them."

"I don't know," Meredith said. "Might be a good morning project. Park somewhere near the school and check that out."

"Good idea," Julia said.

Meredith put the camera back in her bag. "Give me ten minutes, and we can plan our week."

"Julia?" Carmen called. "A woman named Sally Davis is on line one. Can you speak with her?"

"Sure can," Julia said. She waved to Meredith and hit the buttons on the phone to pick up the call. "This is Julia Foley. How may I help you?"

"Hello, ma'am," said a woman's voice, heavy with a thick Georgian accent. "My name's Sally Davis, and I think my granny might be one of the girls in the picture of the five kids that ran in the Savannah paper yesterday."

Julia felt her pulse accelerate. She pulled a legal pad toward her and grabbed a pen. "That's interesting, Miss? Mrs.? Davis."

"Mrs. But call me Sally."

"Sally. What makes you think it's your grandmother?"

"I've got some old photographs of her I think you might want to see. Is there a reward for finding the sister that's still missing?"

"At this point, we're just information-gathering," Julia said smoothly. "Are you in Savannah, Sally?"

"No, I live out in Guyton. Exactly where those babies were photographed. That's where my granny was born too. I'm pretty sure it's her."

"Because…?"

"I might have some old family papers that prove it," the woman on the other end of the line said. "I'll have to see if I can find 'em. You want to come out here and talk?"

Julia grabbed her planner and flipped to the week's work. "Um, how would Wednesday work? Is there a place we could meet?"

Sally Davis rattled off the address of a diner on the main street. Before she hung up, she said earnestly, "I was really hoping there might be a little something to help me take care of my granny. Her money's about gone now, and it's important to me to take good care of her till her time comes."

Julia had barely hung up the phone when Carmen called out again. "Cora Chisholm, line two."

"Got it. Thank you."

Julia punched buttons again and picked up the correct line. "Good morning, Miss Cora. It's Julia. How can I help you?"

"You can help," decreed a voice that clearly wasn't Miss Cora, "by coming over here to Mama's house and explaining what the meaning of this photo in the newspaper is."

"Now, Dolly, there's no need to be rude." Miss Cora sounded unruffled. "Julia, would you and Meredith have time to stop by sometime today?"

"Absolutely," Julia assured her. "How's eleven?"

"I have a luncheon at twelve thirty," said a third female voice, "so it'll have to be brief. But that works for me."

"And me," said the person named Dolly.

"Wonderful. We'll see you soon then." Miss Cora ended the call.

Julia grabbed her notepad and planner and headed for Meredith's office. "We've been summoned," she reported as she entered.

"Summoned?" Meredith's forehead wrinkled.

As Julia explained the conversation she'd just had, Meredith began to nod as if it made sense. "Miss Cora must have told her daughters about that photograph. Dolly's a little older than we are. She can be a bit bossy. The family has gone to First Baptist for generations, and I believe Dolly is very active there. I know Shelby, the younger one, better. I've worked with her on a couple of event-planning committees, and she is generally sweet and helpful."

Julia had never met either daughter. "Dolly didn't sound very happy with us."

Meredith laughed. "Dolly is generally not happy about much of anything, as I recall." And with that, she dismissed the phone call.

"So let's get our plan for the week organized, and then we'll go socialize with Miss Cora and her daughters."

"I've got a meeting scheduled with a woman who thinks her grandmother could be our missing child," Julia said, tapping the planner she'd just opened. "But she hinted that she'd like a reward for the information she claims to have. To pay for her dear old granny's care, she said."

Meredith frowned. "I'm not sure I'm interested in paying someone to be reunited with long-lost family. Doesn't it seem as if that would be reward enough?"

"It does to me," Julia said. "Just thought I'd better confirm that you felt the same way."

Together, the partners worked out a schedule for surveilling both the Pettis residence and Oren Vance, assuming they could catch him leaving work again this week.

"We need to ask Gaye more about his schedule," Meredith said. "She didn't give us much detail."

"We can have Carmen give her a call while we're at Miss Cora's," Julia said. And then she wouldn't need to be involved, which suited her just fine.

Meredith cast her a narrow-eyed look, one eyebrow arching to show that she knew what Julia was thinking. But she nodded. "That works."

Just before eleven, they made the short trip from the office to Miss Cora's, walking along the northern edge of Forsyth under the live oaks that shaded East Gaston Street until they reached the stately Devender-Chisholm House they'd toured less than two weeks ago.

Julia took a deep breath and made a sweeping gesture. "After you."

Meredith grinned. "Chicken."

Together, they mounted the wide, shallow steps to the broad front door of Devender-Chisholm House. Meredith rang the bell. Almost immediately, the sound of frantic yapping followed as tiny paws skittered wildly across the interior tile floor. A little gray poodle pressed its paws against the glass pane in the sidelight on the side of the door.

"That wasn't here the last time we visited," Julia said, looking at the tiny dog that continued to bark its head off.

"Lance, quiet!" An arm swooped down and scooped up the dog, the barking ceased abruptly, and a moment later, the front door opened.

"Hello," said the woman now holding the dog. She wore an elegant cashmere duster in a deep teal with a matching shell beneath and a long strand of pearls, and slim gray wool trousers with ballet flats in soft-looking gray leather. Shifting the little poodle to her left hand, she held out her right, palm up. "Please come in. Hi, Meredith, it's nice to see you."

"You too," Meredith said, smiling. "Have you met my partner, Julia Foley?"

"I have not had the pleasure, but I've heard tons of good things from my husband and his colleagues about your work in juvenile court," the woman said, extending her hand. "Shelby Chisholm Nichols."

Julia shook her hand firmly, noting that although Shelby was pleasant, she had just notified Julia of her considerable social standing. Her husband was both a member of a prestigious law firm and a son of Old Savannah Society, as was Shelby herself. Although the woman had to be close to sixty, by Julia's reckoning, her face looked at least a decade younger and her hair was a lovely blond. "Thank you," Julia said, releasing Shelby's hand. "It's nice to meet you. You too, Lance."

Shelby beamed. "His full name is Lancelot, and he's occasionally loud but essentially harmless. He might lick you to death if you encourage him. Follow me."

Meredith laughed. "Quite a noble name."

Shelby winked. "We thought he needed something to live up to." She turned to lead the way, her smoothly coiffed French twist shining under the refracted light from the chandelier in the entry. "Mama's in the den with Dolly. Come on back."

As she walked, she spoke over her shoulder. "I don't know why Mama's got herself so worked up over this photo, but I'm sure there's some simple explanation for why Grandmama had it in her Bible. I'm glad she asked you to look into it."

Julia and Meredith followed Shelby through the home on a different path than they'd taken on their previous visit. Today, there was no detour through the kitchen but a straight shot back a long hallway and right into the Christmas wonderland of the parlor where they'd visited with Miss Cora before. The tree sparkled with lights, and the mantel glowed with subtle lights wound through a gorgeous garland draped atop it. Once again, there was a fire going in the gas fireplace, and the room was warm.

Miss Cora rose from the same chocolate leather recliner where she'd been sitting the last time the partners had spoken with her.

"Girls. Thank y'all for coming over." Her eyes twinkled. "My daughters—well, mostly Dolly—had some questions about the photo I gave you. I thought it might be best if we all got together for a little chat. Do you both know my daughter Dolly?"

Another woman had risen to her feet at their entry. Shorter than her younger sister, she wore a light blue, cashmere-silk blend cardigan and matching mock turtleneck with a long navy skirt that flowed to her ankles. Her hair was silver and wavy, cut in a fashionable bob. But she wasn't smiling. "I'm Dolly Chisholm Garrett. Meredith, I know you. I don't know you," she said, directing a piercing blue gaze at Julia.

"Mind your manners, dear," Miss Cora rebuked her elder daughter. She performed the introductions with a calm smile, ignoring Dolly's glower. "Come in, have a seat," she invited Julia and Meredith.

The partners took the seats she indicated. Julia couldn't deny that she felt a little like a child being called before the principal, despite Miss Cora's warm welcome and Shelby's smile.

"So, what is the meaning of this photograph appearing in the newspaper?" Dolly asked.

Chapter Seven

"I'VE ONLY EVER SEEN THAT picture once, years ago, but I recognized it right away. I called Mama, thinking it might upset her, and she told me she gave it to you two!" She turned her frown on her mother.

Miss Cora's face was placid. "I'm curious about it," she said. "And I knew Meredith and Julia would be careful about how they investigate it. There's not a word in there that connects that picture to me."

"That's true," Shelby said. "No one knows where they got the photo, Dolly." She looked at the partners. "Do they?"

"No one except for our receptionist, and she'll never mention it to a soul," Meredith assured them.

"We did not intend for the paper to rerun the article," Julia told the three women. "But when I tried to contact the reporter who had run the 1992 article, I learned he had passed away. The woman I spoke with yesterday decided to do this on her own." She took a moment to explain their futile research of all the surrounding counties and told them about the previous rerun of the picture. "I apologize, but I can't fix it. All we can promise you is that at no point will we divulge the way we became involved."

"See?" Miss Cora turned and smiled at her older daughter. "I told you Meredith and Julia were the souls of discretion."

"But Mama," Dolly said, "I don't even understand why that old photograph matters. It's not as if you knew those people."

Julia watched Miss Cora closely. Was it possible she had some inkling that she could be the missing child? Then again, Miss Cora had told them she'd been an only child. She could be telling herself it was as simple as the photograph of unwanted children striking a chord with her mother, especially if she'd wanted more and been unable to fulfill that dream.

The matriarch appeared untroubled by Dolly's criticism. "That picture must have mattered to your grandmama," she replied. "I simply would like to know why."

"Well," Shelby said, "we may or may not ever find out. And I don't think it's going to hurt anything to have it in the paper, Dolly. I won't be surprised if we never hear another thing about it."

Julia feared Shelby could be right. "You were an only child, you said." She directed her comment to Miss Cora, following her train of thought from a moment ago. "Did your parents want more children?"

"Oh my stars, yes, but it wasn't to be," Miss Cora said, nodding. "People didn't talk much about such things back when I was younger, you understand, but Mama told me once she'd lost four babies before I came along. She had a female surgery when I was born, so she never could have more babies."

"Oh, that's so sad," Meredith said.

Julia remained silent, thinking of how difficult that must have been for Miss Cora's mother. Women who couldn't bear children back then probably suffered from well-meant pity and sympathy their whole lives.

"Well, lucky for us, she had you," Dolly said, her severe expression softening as she turned toward her mother. "But I'm glad she's not still living to see that picture in the paper."

Julia decided that it might be prudent not to mention the telephone call she'd had earlier. Why upset the family when she didn't even know if Sally Davis's suspicions about her grandmother were fact or fiction?

She and Meredith sat through several minutes more of social chatter before taking their leave.

Miss Cora beamed at them as they rose. "Thank y'all for doing this. I don't really expect much will come of it, but I can't help but wonder what my mama was thinking."

This time, Dolly was the one to escort them as they made their way to the door. "I hope y'all don't take offense at my concerns," she said as she steamed through the hallway, clearly expecting them to follow in her wake. "Mama's all worked up about that picture. I think she thinks maybe they're some relation to us, but I just can't imagine how. If they were, it would have to be pretty distant. I've done a lot of our family genealogical research, and we can track all my aunts, uncles, and cousins back several generations."

"My late husband's mother was into genealogy too," Meredith said. "It's fascinating to see where we came from, isn't it?"

"My mother's family was Irish," Julia said. "The McErleans came over on one of the first ships from Eire in 1734 and have been here ever since. But she married a Waverly, so I'm an English-Irish combo."

Dolly smiled politely. "How interesting." She extended a hand. "It was so nice to meet you, Julia, and to see you again, Meredith."

She smoothly transferred her handshake to Meredith then opened the front door and held it open with an expectant smile.

"I'm sure we'll see you again soon," Meredith said, just before stepping onto the porch, "when we find out more about that photo for your mother."

"Don't trouble yourselves too much," Dolly said in a sweet voice. "I'm sure she'll forget all about it soon." Her smile had grown rather fixed and steely. "Have a nice day, girls."

The partners descended the steps in silence. It wasn't until they were several paces down Gaston Street from the gracious old home that Julia spoke. "It really doesn't sound like Dolly wants us to learn more about that picture."

Meredith nodded. "Makes you wonder if she already knows something we don't, doesn't it?"

***

Back at the office, Carmen had taken a message for Julia about Beau's Christmas gift. Julia had taken the precaution of having any information about gifts sent to the office rather than her home. She'd ordered a new putter he'd been longing for, and she needed to run out to the pro shop at the Savannah Golf Club and pick it up. She intended to pay cash for it rather than have it put on their account and risk him seeing that she'd made the purchase.

She gathered her things. On the way back, she decided, she'd make a short stop in Parkside. Checking on a person they were surveilling at many different times was good practice. At the last moment, she stashed the small camcorder in her bag as well.

The little bell over the front door rang just as she exited her office to tell Carmen and Meredith where she was going. Smiling, she walked up the hallway past the coffee service. Bright morning light was flooding in the open door, making it hard to see who their caller was, but as she approached, she recognized Gaye Strieter.

"Oh, hello, Gaye," she said. "How can we help you today?"

Gaye smiled. "I was in the area, and I thought I'd stop in for a progress report on my case."

Carmen had returned to the reception area to greet the client. "Hello. Is there anything I can help with?"

Julia shook her head. "Mrs. Strieter is stopping in for a progress report, but thank you."

As Carmen settled at her desk—hopefully to prepare the first week's billable hours, Julia thought uncharitably—she beckoned to Gaye to follow her into Meredith's office.

"Meredith," Julia said. "Gaye has stopped by for a progress report on how we're coming along with the surveillance on Oren Vance. Perhaps you could update her and get the information we were discussing?" She smiled brightly at Meredith, who had pawned Gaye off on her last Monday, and then turned to Gaye. "I'm just on my way out, but I'm sure Meredith can answer your questions."

"Oh. All right." Gaye's voice was small. "Hello, Meredith."

"Have a lovely day," Julia said to her. "Mere, I'll be back before lunch. I'm going to stop by Parkside."

Meredith nodded. "Great. See you then."

As Julia made her escape, she heard Meredith begin an exchange of friendly small talk with Gaye. She felt a teeny pinch of guilt for abandoning the field, but she reasoned she'd spoken with the client last week, and it would be good for Meredith to have a more personal acquaintance with the case as well.

But as she buckled her seat belt, she knew she was rationalizing. She just didn't want to have to spend any more time around her former friend than absolutely necessary.

She made her way to the Savannah Golf Club and followed the drive back, past the stately club to the pro shop.

It took her only minutes to pick up the putter. While she was there, she got a sleeve of balls, a new tweed golf cap in the style she knew Beau liked, and a sweater in a subdued moss shade she thought he'd like for the cooler weather in January and February.

After placing her haul in the back seat, she backtracked into town and headed south across Victory past Daffin Park until she turned onto Fifty-First a few blocks west of the Pettis home. She rather liked the vantage point from the parking space she'd had the other day, but she didn't want to park in front of the same house twice, so she actually drove past her quarry's home and parked farther down the street. Once in the space, she angled her mirrors so she could see her prey more clearly.

The little house looked exactly as it had the last time she'd seen it, but there was no car in the driveway. She picked up her phone and read some of the day's news, checking her mirror frequently to make sure she didn't miss any action at the house behind her. It was eleven twenty, and she wondered how long she should surveil the property. Gaye was surely gone by now, and Meredith had asked Julia if they could catch up some more over lunch since their morning had been interrupted by their visit to Miss Cora's. Ten minutes later, she decided she probably needed to get going.

No sooner had she set her phone back in the cradle on her dashboard than a white Honda sedan rolled slowly down the street and pulled into the Pettis driveway.

Without taking her eyes from the view in the mirror, Julia fumbled in her bag for the camcorder and quickly turned it on. Then she raised it and flipped the viewfinder so she could see and ensure she was recording.

The front door of the house opened, and a woman appeared. It was Hilly Pettis, dressed in a flowing green dress with a matching sweater and a purse slung over one shoulder. She had both crutches in one hand, and she leaned them against the porch rail as she came onto the stoop and turned to lock the door behind her.

"Subject Hilly Pettis appears to be leaving home," Julia intoned. The date and time would be embedded in the video. Then she caught her breath as Hilly picked up the crutches in one hand and walked lightly down the steps and along the short sidewalk to the driveway without a single trace of a limp.

"Why aren't you using those crutches, Hilly?" Julia asked as she watched the woman walk easily around the car and open the back door. Then, remembering she was recording, she clapped her free hand over her mouth. Hilly placed the crutches in the back and then got into the front passenger seat, talking animatedly to the driver.

As the white Honda backed out of the driveway, Julia made a quick decision to follow it for a bit and see where Hilly Pettis and her companion were headed.

Hastily, she grabbed her phone and called the office.

"Magnolia Investigations. This is Carmen. How may I help you?" Carmen's voice was warm and friendly and slightly flavored with her Hispanic accent.

"Carmen, it's Julia. Tell Meredith I filmed Hilly Pettis leaving her home without using her crutches, and now I'm following the car she got into. I'll meet her as soon as I can." The partners had planned to meet for lunch at Maté Factor. The quaint little bakery on East Hall Street was one of their favorite lunchtime getaways.

"Oh, good for you! I'll tell her right away." Carmen ended the call without even a farewell, and Julia turned off the camcorder and put her car in DRIVE so she could follow the white car.

They drove for about fifteen minutes before the car she was following turned right into a shopping center and parked in front of a bridal shop.

Two cars behind the Honda, Julia also turned off the highway but steered toward the rear of the lot and drove on down farther, pulling into a space from which she could turn on the camcorder again. And just in time too, she thought, letting out a small hoot of satisfaction as Hilly got out of the Honda, completely ignoring the crutches she'd stowed in the back. She and her friend strolled leisurely into the bridal shop, and Julia turned off the video again. Part of her wanted to follow the women inside, but she knew she had plenty of evidence, and having the woman become aware that someone was watching her would be a disaster. She texted Meredith. ON MY WAY.

Twenty minutes later, she found parking half a block down from Maté Factor. She was tickled to see that Meredith had just parked two spaces in front of her and was getting out of her own car at the same time.

"Wait for me," she called, hurrying to join her friend.

"Hi. I heard you had a productive surveillance session."

"Woohoo, did I ever!" Julia grinned. "Wait until you see what I caught Hilly Pettis doing. Our client is going to be happy."

Meredith raised her eyebrows. "Caught her cold, did you?" She frowned, brushing aside a lock of hair that had fallen in her eyes. "You know, she produced signed medical paperwork documenting an injury. Remind me to look and see who the doctor is. Either she falsified it, or she got the doctor to do it."

"Either way, someone is in big trouble," Julia said. She pulled out her phone and quickly typed a message. "There. I sent you a text, so when we get back to the office you'll remember to check on that."

The pair stepped onto the lovely patterned brick patio, where stone planters overflowed with hardy pansies and other plants that didn't mind the cooler temperatures, and several wooden tables invited customers to enjoy milder weather. Today there were a few hardy souls sipping hot drinks while they lunched, but Julia thought it was a bit brisk to be sitting outside.

The double wooden doors were flanked by large windows with pretty scallop-edged curtains tied back so passersby could see inside, and burgundy awnings echoed the shade of the benches out front. Aromatic pine wreaths were hung on both doors with burgundy ribbons and matching bows. Julia pulled a door open and held it for Meredith before stepping inside.

A few cozy arrangements of chairs were jammed into the narrow spaces on both sides of the door, green plants were tucked into every available nook and cranny, and the scents of baked goods and the teahouse's signature drinks abounded. "What do you want?" Meredith asked. "I'll get the food if you'll find a table."

"I'll have an egg-and-cheese croissant and a chai latte."

Meredith chuckled. "Breakfast for lunch? I'm dying for a Reuben."

"I see someone leaving upstairs," Julia said, pointing up at the tiny balcony. "I'll grab those seats." She suited action to words, ascended the curving staircase, and sank onto a bench against the wall until the two ladies she intended to replace had gathered their bags, shrugged into their sweaters, and departed.

Julia settled at the table, and Meredith arrived shortly after with their meals. "I couldn't resist the Mayan mocha latte," she said ruefully, then inhaled deeply of her drink. "Mmm."

"And I see some things that weren't in the original order," Julia said, pointing to a blueberry almond scone and a cran-raspberry muffin. "We're going to have to walk back to the office to use up all these calories."

Meredith smiled. "Except we'd have to leave our cars here. We can take a stroll around Forsyth later for a breath of air if we feel a mid-afternoon slump coming on. Now let me see that video you just shot."

Julia fished the camcorder out of her bag and handed it over. "We'll be able to pull some good stills off of there too, I hope."

Meredith turned on the camcorder and took it back to the beginning of the episode. Moments in, she gasped. "She's not using her crutches!"

Julia chuckled. "That was my reaction too. Pretty amazing recovery." She shook out a napkin to cover her lap and picked up her sandwich. "Did Gaye give you any more information about her son-in-law's schedule?" As she took the first bite of her croissant sandwich, she momentarily closed her eyes in bliss.

Meredith turned off the camera and handed it back. Then she placed her own napkin in her lap as she replied. "It was a rather odd encounter, to be honest. She says he doesn't really have much of a routine. But it sure sounds like he does. He works the same hours every day, except for days off. He goes to the gym three mornings a week at the crack of dawn—which I have to say is probably the least likely time for an illicit rendezvous—and he generally goes home as soon as he gets off work. He spends evenings and weekends at home or on family outings or watching the kids if the wife has to go out. She's in the Junior League, and she sings in the church choir, so she's got some commitments. They don't rely on Gaye or his family to babysit a ton. She says it could be someone at work, but when I asked her why she suspects an affair and if her daughter thinks he's stepping out, she was vague and noncommittal. 'You know how men can be,' was the best she could come up with. And honestly, I don't know that all, or even most, men 'can be' like that." She set her sandwich down and made air quotes to emphasize her point.

Julia sighed. "I was hoping for more specificity. So I guess we follow him to the gym a couple of times, double-check the weekend information, and go from there?"

Meredith nodded. "I think so. It's possible he's been trolling the internet and is having a relationship online, which could be why we haven't seen any signs of anything amiss. That would be much more difficult to discern."

Julia knew that was true.

"And I want to know what's going on with you and Gaye as well," Meredith said. "There's something more than 'we just grew apart,' and I want to know what happened. You couldn't get out of there fast enough today."

Julia sighed. "It was a long time ago, and it's not relevant anymore."

Meredith made a scoffing sound and then hastily looked around in chagrin. They both laughed.

But then Julia sighed. "I already told you. Basically, I wasn't up to her standards anymore."

"Did she tell you that?"

"She didn't have to." Julia looked down at her plate. "Our first Christmas break home from college, I called her four times to see when she wanted to get together. She was never home. I could tell her mother was embarrassed that she didn't return my calls. The poor woman was so apologetic. And then I went to a party that she was at. It wasn't a group I normally hung out with, but a boy I knew invited me, and I figured why not. I remember being surprised that she hadn't let me know she'd be going to a party. We always did that type of thing together. She was wearing an outfit that clearly coordinated with a group of her sorority sisters who were there, and she'd lightened and straightened her hair just like theirs. I honestly barely recognized her."

"Did she recognize you?"

Julia felt her mouth twist, and she took a deep breath to smooth out the old, roiling insecurities that she thought she'd shed long ago. "In a manner of speaking. She took one look at me and turned away. She and her giggling posse had quite a bit of fun at my expense. Needless to say, I left the party early."

"Oh, Jules." Meredith stretched a hand across the small table and covered Julia's, and Julia realized she was clenching her fist.

She took another deep breath and made an effort to relax. "Actually, I should probably thank her sometime. I decided to not care about the party scene and became determined to be the girl with the best grades and all the answers." She shrugged. "And along the way, Gaye stopped mattering."

"Until now," Meredith said.

"Well, I can pretty much count on one hand the times our paths have crossed since I came back to Savannah," Julia said. "I've seen her at a couple of parties, but that's about it. I don't have kids and she does, I work and she doesn't, we don't attend the same church, and we're not involved in any of the same organizations…it hasn't been hard."

"You never mentioned her once in college," Meredith said.

"She was my past," Julia said flatly. "I was looking toward the future after that."

Meredith smiled ruefully. "I guess we both changed a lot from freshman year on, but rooming with you senior year was a highlight of my life."

Julia swallowed, turning her hand up to squeeze the one that still covered hers. "Mine too." She dropped her head. "I need to let this go, don't I?"

"I think you might feel happier if you did," Meredith agreed. "But I understand how difficult it is to be forgiving when someone you thought you could count on turns on you like that." She shook her head. "I suspect she regrets it."

"Forgiving her might make me feel better, but it won't change one fundamental fact," Julia said. "She'll never be one of the people I count on again."

Chapter Eight

AFTER SHIFTING TO LIGHTER TOPICS for the rest of the meal, the partners drove their cars back to the office.

After Julia entered her office, set her things down, and took off her sweater, Carmen called from the hallway. "A lady from Springfield emailed us this morning. She's a nurse in a senior care facility, and she thinks one of their residents could be the missing sister from Guyton."

"What's her name?" Julia heard Meredith ask. She quickly hurried to the front hallway to join the discussion.

Carmen was reading from a steno pad on which she'd taken notes. "The lady who emailed is Molly Rose McNitt. The patient's first name is Carrie. She doesn't mention a last name, but she says the woman is eighty-eight years old."

"Eighty-eight. She'd be the right age."

"And that name," Julia said. "Why does this aide think the patient could be our long-lost sibling?"

Carmen consulted her notes again. "She wouldn't say. She wanted to speak with one of you. I asked if she could come into the agency, but she said she doesn't come into Savannah very often. And if you want to meet the old lady, you'd have to go out to Springfield anyway. I have her number here, and the name and address of the senior living facility."

Meredith crossed the hallway and took the piece of paper Carmen offered. "I'll call her and see about setting up a time to visit. I guess we're going to Springfield."

She had her phone in her hand, and it buzzed as she spoke. She glanced at it and then raised it for a better look, smiling. "Oh, look. Chase was in town this weekend. He escorted a friend to a gala yesterday."

She expanded the image on her phone and held it up so Julia and Carmen could see it. In the picture, Chase wore an impeccably tailored gray pinstripe suit with a red Christmas tie, and his arm was around the shoulders of a young woman. Both had big smiles for the camera.

Julia recognized her instantly. It was the same brunette beauty she'd seen him with at the Botanical Gardens Christmas light show—tall, slender, curly hair framing a wide smile in a truly stunning face.

Across from her, Carmen's face was frozen in a noncommittal smile. The phone rang, and Carmen turned away immediately. "I need to get that," she said.

Meredith clicked a button, and the screen on the phone went dark. "Let me make this call and see when we can go to Springfield. I guess we're committed to following up every lead on this, no matter how slim."

"All right." Julia headed for her office and spent the rest of the afternoon catching up on paperwork. She took a spin by the hospital at day's end and followed Gaye's son-in-law, but she had no reason to expect that he'd do anything other than go right home, and he didn't. Ardsley Park at suppertime, when everyone was coming home from work, was not the place to sit in your car and hope to remain unnoticed, so she drove to Daffin Park and hung out in the lot near the playgrounds for fifteen minutes before driving back by the Vance home. Twice. And both times, Oren's car was still parked in the driveway.

***

On Tuesday morning, Carmen bounced into Julia's office before Julia could even set her briefcase down. "*¡Holá, jefa!*"

Julia laughed. "Hello to you too." She was glad to see Carmen's mood was so bright. Maybe she'd imagined it yesterday, and Meredith's picture hadn't upset Carmen. "What's up?"

"I went to the library before I went home yesterday," the young woman said. "It occurred to me that none of us had checked the National Archives."

Julia looked up sharply from unzipping her planner. "I didn't even think of that. Did you find anything?"

"The library has a subscription," Carmen told her, "so I was able to do a free search of the 1930 census data. I found the full names of a family that included a then three-year-old boy named Sumner Denton."

"You found him!" Julia clapped her hands. "Way to go, Carmen!"

Carmen glanced at a piece of paper she carried. "The father was Mason Denton, and the mother was Mildred Denton. At that time there was only one other child, a girl named Roberta Dorothy Denton, born 1929. Sumner would be 93 this year, and she'd be 91, if they're even still living. And the other three would have been born in the first few years of the thirties, if she really did sell them in 1935."

"Roberta Dorothy probably married and doesn't go by Denton anymore," Julia said thoughtfully, "but you just reminded me of something. When Harper told me about Sumner, she tried the phone number she found in the file of information with no luck."

Carmen nodded. "I'll look for it. Can't hurt to try again."

Julia put her things away, booted up her computer, and checked her email.

A few minutes later, she heard Carmen's heels tapping back down the hallway. "I found it," she announced. "The phone number is still connected, but it just rings and rings. It's an Effingham County landline. I checked."

Julia smiled. "Guyton and Springfield are in Effingham. It makes me hope that he didn't go far from his birthplace."

"I tried to search for Roberta Dorothy too," Carmen told her. "But I couldn't find anything. Searching for Roberta D. didn't work either."

"But now we know Sumner is—or was—in Effingham County not so long ago," Julia reminded her. "Great work! Time for a raise."

"I'll take it," Carmen declared, grinning.

As the young woman headed back to the reception area, Julia remembered that she and Meredith needed to discuss a Christmas gift and bonus for Carmen. Quickly, she scribbled a note on her to-do list so she wouldn't forget.

Meredith came in a few minutes later.

Julia eyed her friend with approval. She looked neat and stylish in a khaki-tan pantsuit paired with an ivory shell and a peach scarf that gave the outfit a feminine dash of color.

"Good morning," Meredith said, pausing in Julia's office doorway. "I'm ready for our road trip." She was referring to a trip out to

Effingham County, where she had made an appointment to stop by the nursing home to speak with the attendant who had contacted them, and where Julia had set up a time to speak with Sally Davis, the woman who claimed her grandmother was the child they were seeking.

Julia nodded. "Maybe today is the day we discover Mr. Sumner's sibling."

Meredith smiled wryly. "And then all we'll have to do is locate Mr. Sumner himself."

Julia laughed. "And that."

"First meeting is at eleven," Meredith said. "It's about a forty-five-minute drive, but let's plan on leaving around ten to give ourselves plenty of time. I'm not sure exactly where the nursing home is."

Julia gave her a thumbs-up, and Meredith moved out of her doorway toward the front office she occupied.

An hour later, Julia had just tidied up her desk when Meredith appeared in the doorway again. "Ready to go?"

Julia picked up her purse. It matched her deep gray pumps and the pale blue paisley jacket she'd chosen to wear with gray slacks. "Ready. I can drive if you like."

"Sounds good."

The pair climbed into Julia's vehicle, and she drove out of Savannah, along US 80 and up to Route 21.

Meredith's cell phone rang as they passed the exit for the airport. She pulled it from her bag, then hit the button to answer the call and held the phone to her ear. "Hello, honey."

Julia surmised that the caller was either Chase or Carter, one of Meredith's sons. She tried not to eavesdrop, and let her mind wander to the upcoming appointments as Meredith exchanged pleasantries with the caller, but when her friend asked, "What?" in a tone of voice that sounded distinctly agitated, Julia couldn't help but listen.

"But that's our *Nutcracker* day," Meredith said.

Julia knew that Meredith took Kaden and Kinsley to a local production of *The Nutcracker* at Christmas each year. They came down and stayed overnight and then attended the play. Next Saturday was the date.

Meredith said, "Yes," and "Mm-hmm," a number of times, and when the call ended, she immediately turned to Julia. "Oh, I'm so provoked!"

"What's wrong?"

"One of Sherri Lynn's sisters decided to go on a cruise between Christmas and New Year's, and so now they have to have their family Christmas get-together on a different date—and Saturday the nineteenth is the day they chose. Sherri Lynn tried to tell them that wouldn't work, but they steamrolled right over her. As usual. Never mind the fact that we already had plans for that day." In the passenger seat, Meredith crossed her arms and glowered.

"Oh boy, that's difficult," Julia sympathized. Carter's mother-in-law had died several years ago, and Julia knew that ever since, the siblings had been a bit unmoored. They tended to squabble over small things and blow minor issues out of proportion. She had heard a number of stories about how distressed Sherri Lynn was by their constant bickering.

"I guess I'm going to have to give away my tickets," Meredith said. "The kids are going to be disappointed. They both enjoy our tradition." She sighed. "Know anyone who might like to attend?"

Julia shook her head. "Not offhand, but if someone comes to mind, I'll let you know." She glanced over at her friend, who was looking disconsolate. "I'm sorry."

"I'm sorry too," Meredith said. "For Sherri Lynn. Her brothers and sisters haven't been very fair to her at all since their mom died. They pretty much ignore her wishes, since she's the only one of them who 'moved away.'" She made air quotes with her hands. "They all see each other all the time, yet they act like Charleston is a two-day drive instead of a two-hour one. They never visit her and Carter in Charleston. They always expect them to come here. And Carter says the only time they call her is when one of them gets mad at another one and then tries to enlist her to be on a side. It's like middle school."

"Ugh," Julia said. "Maybe she's better off not living close."

Meredith snorted. "I believe she and Carter both think so." She lapsed into a morose silence.

After a few minutes of quietly driving, Julia cleared her throat. "Hey, we should take a few minutes to discuss Carmen's situation. She's pretty bummed that she had to use money from her car fund to replace her dryer."

"I know," Meredith said. "I'm afraid she's not going to be able to get another car before it gets hot again."

"Christmas is coming," Julia said. "We could give her a generous bonus."

"That's a great idea," Meredith said. "Where is my brain?"

Julia smiled. "On other matters?"

Meredith made a show of dusting off her hands. "Not anymore. Yes, that's a good idea. When we get back to the office, let's take a look at the books and see what kind of bonus we could give her. And also, she's been with us for more than six months now. We could always do a performance review and increase her salary. I think business has been good enough that it would be warranted."

"That's an even better idea," Julia proclaimed. "We should have done a three-month review, I suppose. It just didn't occur to me."

"Me neither," Meredith said. "Being a small business owner is a whole different thing from helping Ron on an occasional basis."

"And I never thought about things like this at all," Julia confessed. "In Atlanta, I didn't own the practice, and here I worked for the county. HR was not even on my radar."

They chatted about inconsequential things during the rest of the drive. As Julia entered the outskirts of Springfield, Meredith pointed ahead. "Isn't that a pretty little church?"

The building in question was clearly historical and painted white with a deep red set of double doors at the top of a small flight of steps. Adjacent to a well-kept cemetery, it looked as if it had been there for over a century.

"I wonder if it's still in use," Julia mused. "So many of those small church buildings have closed as their congregations have dwindled."

"Our church seems to have lost a few families recently," Meredith remarked. "Although we're certainly in no danger of closing the doors."

"Is something unusual going on?" Julia asked. "Ours continues to grow, I believe. We just had a ceremony last week for new members again."

Meredith shook her head. "Nothing particularly unusual. Our new minister is very different from our old one, and I guess there's always some change when a church loses a longtime pastor and has to get used to a new one."

"I'm sure." Was Julia imagining it, or was there a wistful tone in Meredith's voice? Her attention was claimed by a verbal direction from her navigation app on her phone. "Oh, look. The nursing home is just down this street two blocks."

The end of the drive took only a moment, and soon the partners were stepping out of the car. This facility was very different from the one where Delyse lived and where Julia had visited with Baruch Helms.

The building was two stories of white brick with a large columned central entry and a balcony above featuring the same columns. It looked as if it once had been a grand home, years ago in a different time.

Entering the lobby, Julia was a little sad to see that, other than the high ceilings the lovely old place boasted, little was left that hadn't been remodeled. Unlike the very nice facility in which Delyse and Baruch lived, this one seemed a little tired and run-down. The artificial Christmas tree in the corner had a sparse string of colored lights on it and an equally sparse number of Christmas balls in various shades. It was the only sign of holiday cheer in the entire lobby, and calling the poor old tree with its oddly bent limbs "cheerful" was a kindness.

"Hello," said the woman at the desk. "How may I help you?"

"We're here to speak to Molly Rose McNitt about a patient," Julia told her.

"I'll page Molly Rose," the receptionist said. She pushed a registration book toward them and handed each of them a visitor badge. "Please sign in and wait here."

Ten minutes and more passed before they heard a click from the double doors at the end of a short hallway. A petite woman wearing eye-popping pink scrubs with her dreadlocks bundled back in a net headed toward them, smiling broadly. "Hi, y'all. Thanks for coming out."

Julia and Meredith introduced themselves.

Then Julia asked, "So what is your patient's name, and why do you believe she may be one of the children in the picture?"

"Her name's Carrie Tillman, but her maiden name was Burnsed. She's eighty-eight years old, just the age your missing girl would be, and I've seen pictures of her when she was younger. She had blond hair and she still has blue eyes, and it looks like all those kids in the picture were little blonds." She turned and began to lead the way back toward the double doors. "Follow me, and I'll introduce you to her."

Meredith exchanged a look with Julia, and Julia could tell she was thinking the exact same thing: *We drove out here because this lady thinks there's a resemblance to an eighty-some year-old photo?*

Just beyond the double doors the nurse's aide turned right and walked down a hallway past several patient rooms. At the far end, the hallway turned left, but there was a small lounge in the corner with a tabletop tree that was just about as haphazardly decorated as the one in the lobby. A shrunken little lady in a wheelchair was seated there. She was nicely dressed in a blue blouse with a bow tied at the neck, a navy cardigan, and navy slacks, and there was an ivory afghan over her lap. Her blue eyes were bright, and they lit with interest when Molly Rose approached her.

"Miss Carrie, you have visitors," she informed her patient.

"For me?" The little woman cocked her head like a bird. She had white hair closely cropped in curls that stood out around her pink scalp. "Why, hello, do I know you?" She looked a bit puzzled. "I'm so sorry, but it seems I've forgotten a lot of folks I used to know."

"We've never met before," Meredith said gently, smiling.

"Miss Carrie, this is Julia Foley, and this is Meredith Bellefontaine from Savannah. They'd like to ask you a few questions about your life."

"Well, all right," Carrie Tillman said. "I've lived a long time. Don't know how I can help you, but I'm happy to try."

Meredith smiled and perched on a chair close to the wheelchair. "Mrs. Tillman, I understand your maiden name is Burnsed?"

"That's right. Been Tillman since I was eighteen years old when I married my Eason. He passed two years ago, you know." Her wizened features clouded. "I think it was two years ago. Was it two years, Molly Rose?"

Molly Rose nodded. "You got it right, honey."

The little woman's expression lightened. "He was a good man."

"I'm sure he was," Meredith assured her. "Where did you live when you were a child, Mrs. Tillman?"

"Guyton," the older lady said promptly.

Julia felt a tingle of excitement zip up her spine.

"Was your family from Guyton?" Meredith continued.

"Oh, yes," she said. "I was a Burnsed, you know. Lived there all my life."

"Were your parents also from Guyton?"

Mrs. Tillman nodded again. "My mama and daddy were both born in Effingham and lived in Guyton all their lives."

"Did you have any sisters or brothers, Mrs. Tillman?"

"Two brothers and a sister," she said. "They're all still living, but I don't see them much these days. Mama and Daddy are gone now, of course."

"We're searching for a lady who was from Guyton who may have been adopted," Julia told her.

"Oh, well, I was adopted," Mrs. Tillman said matter-of-factly.

Chapter Nine

CARRIE TILLMAN WAS ADOPTED! JULIA was intrigued. She could see that Meredith felt the same.

In the corner where she was waiting, listening, Molly Rose nodded vigorously, and Julia suddenly realized the nurse must have known. *That* was the reason for her phone call, not simply because of a physical resemblance.

"Are you certain?" Julia asked the elderly lady gently.

"Why, yes. Mama told me I was." Mrs. Tillman sounded calm and assured.

"Do you know who your birth parents were?"

The older lady shook her head, making the curls dance. "No idea. We never talked about it much."

"Were you curious at all?"

Mrs. Tillman shrugged. "I had a good home, a good family. What did it matter who those other people were?"

It seemed an astounding lack of curiosity to Julia. She couldn't imagine not wanting to find out who'd borne her, who'd contributed to her DNA, if she learned she was adopted. But Mrs. Tillman had been raised in an era when that kind of thing wasn't discussed much and indeed, any reference to it had probably been actively discouraged. She may have convinced herself that it didn't matter, and who was Julia to say it did? After all, wasn't a family's love far more important?

"Mrs. Tillman, do you have a birth certificate?" Julia asked. Her heart was beating fast. Could this really be the woman from the picture? And if so, how was she connected to Miss Cora's deceased mother?

The old woman paused. "Of a sort," she finally said. "My parents had to send away for one when I started school because I didn't have one before that."

Suspicion rose. Even in 1932, many people had birth certificates. It was possible the infant Carrie had been born at home and no birth certificate had been registered...but wasn't it convenient that she had no birth certificate? If Julia was a betting woman, she'd bet that the Burnseds had falsified Carrie's birth certificate. Or they'd known she didn't have one.

The news made it much less likely that they'd learn anything of use from the birth certificate. Still, they needed to cross all the *t*'s. "Would it be possible for us to see the one you have?"

"I can ask my daughter," Carrie offered. "She keeps all that stuff for me now."

"That would be helpful," Meredith said. She pulled out a slim, gray leather business card case and extracted one of the agency's cards. "Would you please ask her to send us a copy if she wouldn't mind?"

"I'm sure that would be fine." Mrs. Tillman took the card and held it close to her face so she could read the information. Then she extended it in a trembling hand to Molly Rose. "Would you take care of that for me until we get back to my room, please?"

"I'd be happy to, Miss Carrie." Molly Rose took the card and stored it in a pocket of her uniform. "I can take a picture of it, and we can send it to your daughter on the computer if you like."

"That would be lovely." Mrs. Tillman beamed. "My daughter lives in Macon, so I don't see her very often. I'm so lucky to have Molly Rose here. She keeps me straight."

"We keep each other straight," Molly Rose said, grinning. "I'm gonna show these ladies out now, Miss Carrie, and then I'll take you to get ready for lunch."

"Thanks for coming out," Molly Rose said to Meredith and Julia as she led them to the front of the building. "Isn't she a sweet soul?"

"She is," Julia agreed. "Thank you for contacting us."

Back in the car, Julia and Meredith looked at each other. Julia said, "Well. That was a bit of a bombshell."

Meredith laughed. "I think Molly Rose did that on purpose. Not telling us Carrie Tillman was adopted, I mean."

Julia chuckled. "Yes, I think so too. She enjoyed her little surprise."

"Do you think she really could be Sumner Denton's missing sister?"

"I think it's as much of a possibility as Miss Cora is." Julia mulled it over. "She's from the right area, she's the right age, she's adopted. Or perhaps she was bought." She pulled out of the parking lot. "Next up, we're meeting Sally Davis for coffee in Guyton. She's the one who says her grandmother is our girl."

The drive to Guyton took only about ten minutes. The moment they walked into the little diner, a woman popped up from a booth near the back and waved. "Are you the Savannah detectives?"

Every person in the place turned and looked at them.

"Ah, we're the investigators," Julia said as they approached. She extended a hand. "Are you Sally?"

"Sure am." The woman was short and wide, with dark red hair that curled wildly to her shoulders. She was wearing bright blue eyeshadow of a sort that Julia had forsworn over forty years ago, and it clashed alarmingly with her green eyes. Freckles liberally dotted every exposed inch of skin. She positively exuded bouncy energy.

Julia introduced herself and Meredith. They slid into the booth across from Sally. "So," Julia said, "tell us why you believe your grandmother might be the girl in the picture."

Sally had a copy of the photo that had run in the paper, and she pushed it across the table. Stabbing a finger at the children, she said, "This girl looks just like my granny did when she was little."

She pulled an envelope from a giant bag crammed into the corner of her booth. "See this? Look here." She spilled a number of photographs across the table and grabbed one. "Doesn't this look just like that little girl? This is my granny."

Julia, more or less forced into action, accepted the photo and studied the picture. The child appeared to be light-haired and light-eyed, and she had curls like the toddler in the photo. But it was impossible to discern any real resemblance. "How old is she? Do you know her birthday and the year she was born?"

"May 27, 1932," Sally said. "Same year as the girl you're looking for."

"And how does she know her birthdate?"

Sally looked puzzled. "What do you mean?"

"Does she have a birth certificate?"

"I don't know. Probably. Doesn't everybody? I guess her parents just told her when her birthday was."

Meredith made notes on a legal pad as Julia conducted the interview.

Julia picked up another photo and looked at it. "Which photo is the earliest one? Do you know?" She flipped over one after another. A few were dated, and one or two had names scribbled on the back, but none that she'd heard.

Sally shuffled through the photographs. "This one, maybe? I'm not really sure."

The one she offered showed a plump toddler with sparse light hair and light eyes, probably blond and blue if the photo had been done in color. She wore a plaid dress with a lacy white collar, a full skirt, and what looked like a crinoline peeping out beneath it. She had on the boxy little white leather shoes so common in that day and lacy white anklets. A diaper sagged below the hem of the dress. She stood with one fat little hand steadying herself beside a brick wall. Tiny white teeth gleamed in a joyous smile.

Meredith took the photo from her and flipped it over, looking at the back, but there was no writing on it. "This child looks much younger than three," she said, a clear note of doubt in her voice. "Maybe eighteen months, if that."

Sally frowned. "I'm sure she must be three. That's the age the little girl was sold, right? Maybe she's a young three, or just not quite three."

"Do you have any other documentation?" Julia asked. "Any other reason you believe your grandmother is the missing child?"

"Well, people always said she didn't look anything like the rest of the family."

Julia started to speak and then stopped. Again, she said, "Is there a birth certificate or any documentation that would lead us to believe your grandmother is the Denton child?"

"I'll have to check," Sally said vaguely. "You said something about a reward?"

"No, we did not," Julia began. "We—"

"Just a small consideration," Sally interrupted. "Seein's how I'll be doing you a favor digging through my granny's papers. How about I call you when I get some things together, and that'll give you time to get the money arranged?"

Meredith cleared her throat. "We can discuss that," she said. "Julia and I have to get back to Savannah now. Why don't you call us if you find anything concrete to establish that your grandmother is the missing child?"

"That sounds like a plan." Sally beamed and slid out of the booth, dragging the large tote with her. "I'll give y'all a call."

Meredith and Julia sat in silence for a moment as Sally bustled off.

"Well." Julia reached for her purse and rose. "I have a strong feeling that woman is attempting to scam us."

Meredith nodded, sliding along the bench until she too could stand. "I have a strong feeling you are right."

Back at the office, Julia had about an hour to catch up on paperwork before she had to leave for a hair appointment.

Since returning to Savannah, she'd gotten her hair cut regularly at Charlton Street Snips, a small salon whose owner she had known since grade school. The salon was located on the ground floor of a lovely historic building on East Charlton Street in the historic district. Steps swept up on either side of the entrance to a balcony.

Julia opened the glass-fronted door with its holly and pine wreath and stepped down two shallow stone steps into the salon. She stood in a foyer area, around which were situated three alcoves with salon stations. Only one was in use today.

"Hi, honey," chirped Maisie Fellows, a tiny bleached blond in a smock over black jeans and a black T-shirt. Maisie was Julia's age, but Julia didn't think anyone would peg them as classmates. Maisie dressed in youthful fashions, streaked her hair with vibrant shades of red, blue, pink, or green, depending on the season, and kept her five-foot-nothing frame in top condition. Today's hair color was a deep Christmas green. "I'll be with you in a sec. Just let me get Verona under the dryer."

She guided the woman at her station back to a set of chairs with dryer hoods and set the heat to the level she wanted. Then she briskly swept the floor around the station before beckoning to Julia. "Okay, your turn." She made a critical survey of Julia's hair as she led her to the shampoo station and swirled a cape around her neck. "Whoops. No more waiting six weeks for you. That's a little out of hand."

Julia laughed. "Yes, four-and-a-half to five works much better." They were silent for a few minutes as Maisie shampooed and conditioned Julia's hair, giving her a delightful scalp massage in the process. When she was finished, she ushered Julia back over to her station.

"So whatcha have goin' on?" Maisie loved nothing better than to hear about Julia's cases, and as long as no names were mentioned, Julia didn't mind sharing a few generalities.

"I saw the picture in the paper that asked folks to contact you," Maisie informed her. "I bet that brought out the wing nuts."

Julia laughed. "Maybe one. We haven't really learned anything concrete that would help us yet. We picked up two more clients recently. A suspicious spouse, and a lawn-care company."

"Oh, which one?" Maisie asked. Then she smacked herself on the forehead. "Sorry. I know you can't say, but I bet it's about some client suing them for wrecking their yard or something." She began to snip expertly. "I don't know any lawn-care companies anyway except Swann. My brother-in-law works for them."

How coincidental would it be if he knew Hilly Pettis? "Janey's husband? I don't think I knew that."

Maisie nodded. "He's been there for at least ten years. They do a nice job, if you're ever looking for someone."

"We might be. What's his name? I can't remember...Benny Crites?"

"That's it," Maisie said. "I think I have a couple of their company cards—remind me to give you one before you leave."

"I've heard they do a good job." Julia's brain was racing, trying to find some way to keep Swann Lawnscapes in the conversation and perhaps learn a little more. "I've met the owner. Is it a big place?"

"No, they employ about twenty people, I guess." Maisie did some light layering around the back of Julia's head. "One of their office gals is off right now with a bum ankle, but Benny says he heard she was faking."

Julia laughed. "Why would you fake a bad leg for an office job? Seems like she could still do the work sitting down."

"I guess she does a lot of running in and out, trying to find the boss, stuff like that. Benny says she got some doctor, a high school friend of hers, to write a letter saying she got hurt, but that was a load of mulch, if you know what I mean."

"Wow," Julia said. "Sounds like Benny should be an investigator." She didn't want to alert Maisie to her interest in Swann Lawnscapes, so she decided to turn the conversation into less tricky channels. "So does your family still get together for Christmas?"

Maisie accepted the pivot easily, unaware that she'd just handed Julia quite a windfall. "Yes, we all go to church together on Christmas Eve, and Janey and I have taken turns hosting Christmas dinner ever since our folks passed away."

The rest of the appointment was uneventful. With her hair freshly trimmed and blown dry, Julia wished Maisie a happy holiday and hurried out to the car. She tried to call Meredith, but her friend had already left the office.

Julia made herself some notes and decided the rest could wait until tomorrow. It had been a busy day. Time to head home.

***

On Wednesday morning, Julia stopped at Back in the Day Bakery on Bull Street on her way to the office for some of their signature cinnamon swirls. Meredith and Carmen might complain about the calories, but they adored the occasional treats, and Julia liked to surprise them every now and again.

As she was stepping away from the Tiffany-blue counter with her purchase in a heavenly smelling bakery bag, someone called her name. "Julia Foley!"

Julia hid a wince. She had immediately recognized the stentorian tones of Miss Cora's older daughter, Dolly Garrett. Fixing a smile on her face, she turned. Dolly sat halfway down the narrow room at a table in front of the big windows, two other women with whom Julia had a nodding acquaintance seated with her.

Julia greeted each of them and then smiled at Dolly. "How's your mother?"

"Mother's wonderful. May I have a word?" Dolly surged up out of her seat, and to Julia's surprise, caught her elbow and towed her several yards away. "I don't want anyone overhearing us," Dolly said in a low voice. "Have you learned anything else about that photograph?"

Julia shook her head. "We've had a few people contact us, but nothing's panned out yet." Which was absolutely true. She had no intention of explaining their every move to Dolly.

Dolly sniffed. "A wild goose chase, just as I expected. I thoroughly disapprove of you dragging Mother into this, you know."

Julia refrained from reminding the woman that said dragging had been the other way around. She stared at Dolly. "Thank you for letting me know." There was a thread of prosecutorial steel in her tone, and as she had hoped, it registered.

Dolly flushed. "I just don't want Mother upset," she muttered. "I really wish you'd just let this go."

"Your mother hired us," Julia pointed out. "If we find nothing, then that's what we'll report to her. Now if you'll excuse me, I must be going." She turned on her heel and headed for the door. She strode along Bull Street to where she'd parked her car beneath the shade of a live oak.

When she reached the office, she tossed her things on her desk and carried the bakery bag to Meredith and Carmen, both of whom had already arrived. As they dug into the tasty treat, Julia shared the encounter with Dolly Garrett.

Meredith stopped, her cinnamon bun halfway to her mouth. "That woman!" she exclaimed. Then she smiled. "It sounds as if you put her in her place, which is probably not a feeling she's accustomed to. Oh, I wish I'd been there."

Julia smiled. "Well, I didn't actually intend to get snippy, but she got my back up with her demand that we stop investigating. As I said in so many words, she didn't hire us, and she can't fire us."

Carmen smiled, dark eyes sparkling. "Thank goodness. I'm invested in finding the missing sister now. I hope one of these new leads yields some new information."

"Oh! Speaking of new information, I found something out about Swann Lawnscapes I think we might find useful, entirely by accident, when I got my hair cut yesterday." Julia related what Maisie had told her about her brother-in-law working for Kenny Swann and his complaint about the shirker.

As she spoke, Carmen grabbed a legal pad and scribbled notes. "So, this Benny says the slacker went to high school with a doctor who signed a form saying she'd hurt herself?"

"Right."

Meredith grinned. "And we have the medical information with the doctor's signature on it, so now all we need to do is prove the doctor and Hilda Pettis have a relationship."

"But how?" Carmen asked.

Julia rubbed her hands together. "First, we look at Hilly again, find out where she went to high school. I'm pretty certain one of the library branches keeps all the local high school yearbooks, so if we know about how old she is, and we know the doctor's name, we should be able to find them in the yearbook and prove that, at the very least, they've known each other for years."

"We can also google them separately and together," Carmen added. "You never know, maybe something will pop up. I'd be happy to do that."

"Great idea," Julia said.

Carmen cleared her throat. "I took a phone call just before you came in that I haven't even had a chance to tell Meredith about."

Both Julia and Meredith gave her their full attention, alerted by the suppressed excitement in her tone.

"A man called," Carmen said. "He says his father grew up in Guyton and remembers a classmate he went to school with who supposedly was sold. His father lives with him, and he invited both of you to visit and speak with him if you like." She extended a piece of paper, and Meredith practically snatched it from her.

"If we like! Of course we like. I'll return the call," she said to Julia. "Sounds like we'll be making another trip to Guyton."

Julia clapped her hands together. "Another lead," she said happily. "I'm starting to think we may just be able to find out more about that picture."

The Interview, Part 3

Interview with my great-grandfather Sumner Denton, age 93, Guyton, GA 10/12/2020.

Interviewer: *So, let's talk about your years in the army.*

SD: I enlisted in October of 1943. Mrs. Healy died, and I didn't have anywhere to go. So I figured I might as well go fight the enemy. I was only sixteen, but the recruiters didn't know it. I was big for my age, and of course I didn't have a birth certificate or any paperwork. I got sent to boot camp at Fort Benning. That was an experience. All those boys whining about how hard it was. Way I was raised to work, boot camp didn't seem so bad. As soon as I got out of there, I was assigned to the 34th Infantry Division, and I was stuck on a ship with my first platoon and floated over to Europe where they dumped us on the beach at Anzio.

Interviewer: *Were you scared?*

SD: I was too young and dumb to be as scared as I should have been. I was proud to be part of the 34th. They'd just done a bang-up job at Monte Cassino, but they'd lost about eighty percent of their troops, so they brought the division back for a rest and restocked with a bunch of fresh recruits.

Interviewer: So what happened when you landed?

SD: The landing went all right, but it wasn't long before we were fighting Germans on all sides. Like to fainted away the first time I felt a bullet part my hair! Down I dropped, and I fired right back. I kept on firing, and our line advanced. Figured I'd better stick with them, so I just did what everybody else was doing. They called it Bloody February, and it was. Don't know how many men we lost, but it was too many. We were stuck on the beach for pretty near two months before we moved out. It took until June, but we finally freed Rome from the Germans.

Interviewer: Did you ever think about dying?

SD: All the time. I reckon we all did. I was really sad to think that I might die and never get a chance to track down my last living sister. Everybody wrote letters so our families would know we were thinking about them, and sometimes we got letters from home too. My little brother Burdie was fourteen years old and in every letter I got from him, he was making noises about running off and joining up like I did. I prayed the war would end before that happened. One day I got a letter from Burdie with bad news. Our sister Bobbie Dee ran off and got married. She was sixteen years old, and she took off with some boy from the next farm over. Burdie said he couldn't stand it at the farm anymore, and he was going to take off too. He said he'd write, but he never did. And after the war when I went back home on leave, I couldn't find either one of them.

Interviewer: So, you lost touch with your brother and sister who were left? But I thought—

SD: Just hold your horses, boy. I didn't say I never found 'em again, did I?

Chapter Ten

JULIA AND MEREDITH CONFERRED ABOUT Gaye Strieter's case shortly before lunch.

"I got there really early on Monday and again today," Meredith volunteered, "but he was at home until he left for the hospital. And when he left, the wife kissed him goodbye at the door."

"I don't think he's cheating on her," Julia said. "Did Gaye give you anything more specific the last time you met with her?"

Meredith shook her head. "She just said she had a feeling. But I spoke to someone who works in the hospital yesterday, and she said no one there has ever heard anything bad about Dr. Vance. Everyone likes him, and by all accounts he's devoted to his family." She paused. "I think you should speak to her, Jules. Every time I've seen her, she's asked where you are."

Julia rolled her eyes. "All right. But I'm going to tell her I think she's wasting our time."

"I think she may be," Meredith agreed. "But I'd like to know why. She's spending a pretty penny to find out nothing."

The tapping of heels on the glossy floor of the foyer was momentarily muffled as Carmen crossed the large rug they'd laid there. But then it resumed as she approached the doorway of Meredith's office, where the partners sat.

"Knock, knock," Carmen said through the open door. "I have that Sally Davis character on hold. She says she's got some papers for you, and she'll trade them for the reward." She frowned. "What reward?"

Julia laughed. "The reward she insists we're paying, even though we've told her we're not."

"What would you like me to tell her?"

"Tell her we'll call her and let her know when we're coming to Guyton again," Meredith advised. To Julia, she said, "We need to speak with the man who remembers a child being sold, so we have to make the drive anyway."

Carmen gave a thumbs-up and headed back across the hall to her desk.

Just as Julia started to head to her own office, the front door opened, the little bell above it trilling merrily. A woman close to her own age entered. She had what looked like home-dyed blond hair, and she wore all black. "Are you Julia Foley or Meredith Bellefontaine?" she asked in a tone Julia could only characterize as aggressive. She held a small card—one of their business cards, from the look of it—in her hand, and she peered at it as she recited the names.

"I'm Julia Foley." Julia retraced her steps, reaching the foyer just as Meredith came to the door of her office. Julia shook hands with the woman and then introduced Meredith. "And you are…?"

"I'm Tracy Bedford. My mother is Carrie Tillman, and I am here to correct some misconceptions I believe you may have about her."

"Would you like to have a seat?" Meredith invited, indicating her office.

Tracy Bedford followed her into the room, and Julia paused in the doorway. "Would you care for tea or coffee or bottled water?"

"No, thank you," the woman said. "I have another appointment shortly." She held up a manila folder. "I have my mother's birth certificate here."

Julia came in and took a seat. "Thank you for taking time to see us," she said. "Are you aware that Ms. McNitt contacted us, not the other way around?"

Tracy brushed that aside with an irritated flip of her fingers. "Yes, that fool Molly Rose finally confessed what she'd done when I asked Mom where she'd gotten your card and why you wanted her birth certificate." Then she sighed. "I'm sorry. That's not fair. Molly Rose treats Mom so well. We really appreciate her. And I'm sure she thought she was doing the right thing, but...well, let me back up."

She opened the envelope and pulled out a black-and-white copy of a family photo. "This was my grandmother's family when she was a teenager. She was the oldest of four. A girl, two boys, and another girl. My grandmother, Eleanor Booth, was the oldest, and the youngest girl, Teenie, they called her, for Antonia, was eight years younger than Grandmama was." She passed over the image, which Julia accepted. "Eleanor married young and went to nursing school. She was working as a nurse when her mother told her Teenie had gotten herself 'in the family way.' Teenie was only fifteen, and the father of the child didn't stick around long enough to marry her or even find out he was going to be a father. So they sent Teenie away to a home for unwed mothers, and when the baby was born, my grandparents adopted it. That baby was my mother Carrie." She pulled a set of papers from the folder. "Here is my mother's original birth certificate and the amended one that her parents had made."

Julia passed the photo to Meredith and took the papers. Sure enough, on the first one, the mother's name was listed as Antonia Booth and there was no father's name. On the second one, Eleanor B. Wallace and Geoffrey Wallace were listed as the parents.

Julia opted for diplomacy. "That was a kind thing to do. There was a huge stigma attached to being an unwed mother or a child born out of wedlock in that generation. Even when we were growing up, that would have been scandalous."

"But there's more to it than that." Tracy leaned forward. "My mother doesn't know that her aunt was actually her mother."

"Oh my." Meredith winced. "Tracy, we are so sorry to dredge all this up."

Tracy sighed. "It's not your fault. My grandmother died some years ago, and I'm the oldest grandchild. Before she passed, she told me the story and gave me these papers, but she asked me never to tell my mother unless, you know, there would be some reason." She shrugged. "So I've never told her. I imagine, given the age Mom is now, she'll never need to know."

Julia was touched, and she could see that Meredith was too. It must have been difficult for Tracy's grandmother to share the story, given the social mores of the time. But she'd been thinking of her child, who was also her niece, and other descendants, and she'd wanted to make sure someone knew the true circumstances of Carrie's birth.

Julia swallowed. "Thank you for sharing this with us, Tracy. I'm so sorry if this has distressed you. We certainly never intended that, and I'm sure if Molly Rose knew, she would feel the same way. She appears to genuinely care for your mother."

"Can you maybe just tell her you've discovered something that makes you certain Mom is not that missing child?" Tracy asked. "I hope I'll never need to burden her with this ancient history. My grandparents gave her a good life, and I think she's satisfied with that."

"Absolutely," Meredith assured her. "We can tell her exactly that, and if she asks for details, we'll just tell her it's confidential to our investigation."

"Thank you." Tracy briefly closed her eyes. "Thank you so much."

***

At lunch, Julia took a spin by the hospital. As she had anticipated, Oren Vance's black SUV was in the lot where he habitually parked. She found a space not far away and ate a chicken, bacon, and gouda wrap with a side of fried pickles from the 5 Spot in Habersham Village in her car. While she scrolled through social media, she kept one eye peeled just in case Dr. Vance took an unexpected midday break.

Unfortunately, Dr. Vance never moved from the hospital. She sighed. She was going to be forced to speak with Gaye. A thought in the back of her mind struggled for attention, and she allowed it to surface. Meredith's words from their lunch at Maté Factor returned. *I understand how difficult it is to be forgiving when someone you thought you could count on turns on you like that.* Somehow, that simple affirmation had taken some of the bitterness out of Julia's old hurt. She hadn't been silly to feel so devastated. But perhaps it was time to stop allowing it to dictate her life. Look how she'd been avoiding Gaye—there no longer seemed to be such a point to that.

Back at the office, Meredith found her shortly after she returned. "Want to go back out to Guyton this afternoon? I spoke with the son who invited us to come speak to his dad, and around three would work."

"Sure," Julia said. "We can ask Carmen to call Sally Davis and have her meet us again."

"Sounds good," Meredith said.

Suddenly a voice they knew and loved hollered, "Woohoo!" so loudly that it echoed through the old building.

"What on earth?" Meredith asked, grinning.

A second later, Carmen bolted into the room. "Guess what?" She didn't give them a chance to answer. "I found out some things about the doctor," she announced.

"Dr. Tannen, the one who certified that Hilly Pettis injured herself?" Julia asked.

"Right." Carmen nodded. "His full name is Dr. Andrew Tannen, and he's a family physician associated with the Candler system." St. Joseph's/Candler was one of two large Savannah hospitals. Memorial, where Dr. Oren Vance worked, was the other. Candler was the second oldest continuously operating hospital in the United States, having been chartered in 1804. "But," she added, "that information was easily available. Here's the part I had to dig for. Dr. Tannen went to high school here in Savannah, as did Hilly Pettis. And they were in the Thespian Club together."

"Bingo!" Meredith crowed. "So they did know each other."

"Old buddies," Julia added.

Carmen nodded. "There was a picture in the yearbook of them in a play together their senior year. So we can definitely prove there was a prior connection."

"Why don't you call Kenny Swann," Julia said to Carmen, "and see if he can stop by. Either in the next hour or so, or tomorrow. If that works better for him."

"On it." Carmen turned and left the room.

"So next step," Meredith said. "We tell Kenny Swann about Hilly's extracurricular activities and see how he wants to handle this."

"I know how I'd handle it," Julia said. "I'd call Hilly in and show her what we found. Force her to withdraw her claim."

"Or just turn it all over to law enforcement," Meredith said. "Both Hilly and that doctor could be in big trouble."

"I guess it depends on how mad Kenny is," Julia said.

Carmen came back across the hall. "Prepare to present," she said. "Kenny is coming right over."

"Oh my." Meredith scurried to her desk and began shuffling papers. "Julia, have you downloaded that video?"

Julia nodded. "Let me get my laptop. I have it all ready to go, and I also have a flash drive we can give Kenny with all the stills and videos we took."

"Terrific." Meredith continued organizing as Julia headed for her office to retrieve the flash drive.

She made a few notes in Oren Vance's file about the fruitless lunchtime surveillance as well as adding the latest report from their contact in the hospital. Then she heard the tinkling of the bell over the door. As she'd expected, it was Kenny Swann.

Meredith was already greeting him and showing him into the conference room.

"So what have you got for me? Hello, Julia." Kenny extended a hand. He wore khaki pants and a light blue button-down shirt, a casual look that would serve him in the office or on a job site. He struck Julia as being perfectly comfortable in either setting.

"Kenny." She shook the offered hand and indicated a chair. "Please have a seat."

"This sure didn't take long," he said. "I hope you didn't call me over here to tell me you haven't found anything. Because the longer I think about it, the more convinced I am that there's not a thing wrong with Hilly Pettis."

Julia had her laptop already cued up, and she brought it over and set it on the table in front of Kenny. "We've been watching her since the day you first came in. This is from yesterday." She pressed PLAY, and images of the scene Julia had recorded appeared.

Within seconds, Kenny's mouth dropped open. His face darkened. "I knew it," he growled. "What a lazy—" He stopped abruptly, looking sheepish, apparently realizing that his next words were not fit for the company of ladies. "Woman," he finished.

"Exactly," Meredith said, nodding.

"But she had a doctor's diagnosis," Kenny said.

"Yes. Well, we've learned that Dr. Tannen and Hilly went to high school together and were in the same theater club. So we suspect they knew each other reasonably well," Julia said. She handed across a large manila envelope. "Here's a copy of our invoice, our notes on exactly what we did during the course of the investigation, a flash drive with all the photographs and videos we took, and several enlarged copies of frames from the video that show Hilly walking."

But to her surprise, Kenny didn't move to accept the items immediately. "I'd like you to be present when I tell her what you found. Would you be willing to attend a meeting at my office tomorrow?"

"Sure," Meredith said. "But why?"

"Witnesses," Kenny said succinctly. "This woman was willing to enlist a friend to tell me bald-faced lies about an injury so she could collect disability and have time off. I'd like to play this video in front of you, so there's no chance she can try to wriggle out of it. I want her to know there's not a chance she can get away with this."

"What about the doctor?" Meredith asked. "Are you going to report him?"

To her surprise, Kenny shook his head. "Probably not. I don't have time to file a bunch of paperwork and get tangled up in a bureaucratic mess, which is what would happen if I did. And besides, I bet he'd just get a slap on the wrist anyway. Not worth my time."

Julia disagreed, and she could see that Meredith did too, but it wasn't their decision. They had been hired to gather information for a client, and they'd done their job.

Kenny had opened the envelope and checked out the invoice on top of the stack of papers. "That's all?" he asked.

"All what?" Meredith asked.

"Your fee," he said. "I thought it would be a lot larger."

Meredith smiled. "We only charge the hourly fee you were quoted and any additional expenses. In this case, it didn't take very long to catch your employee in the act, and we had very few expenses other than a little gas and that flash drive in your folder."

Kenny rose and shook hands first with Meredith and then Julia. "Ladies, I can't thank you enough. I'll make an appointment with your girl to come back tomorrow, and I'll have Hilly meet us at my office."

As he left the room and headed across the hall, Meredith smiled wryly at Julia. "Our 'girl' will set him straight if she overheard that."

Julia laughed. "I think she was on the phone, so he may live to see another day."

Meredith's smile faded. "It doesn't sit right with me that he's willing to let Andrew Tannen off."

"I know. Me neither, but I'm afraid he's right about the bureaucracy and paperwork. And he probably would just get a slap on the wrist, as Kenny said. Let's give that some thought."

After retrieving their jackets and purses from their offices, the partners took Meredith's car and rode back out to Guyton for yet another set of interviews.

First, they drove to a new address, the residence of Steven Marris, the man who had contacted them to say that his father knew a child who had been sold.

Downtown Guyton was a blink-and-you'll-miss-it small Southern village with numerous newer developments scattered throughout the former farmland around it. The Marris home was in one such development, a large cream-colored brick house with a three-car garage and a long driveway. One of the garage bays was open, and they could see a large riding mower and a golf cart parked there.

They were only halfway along the front walk toward the shaded porch when the door opened and a man stepped out, a sturdy Rottweiler beside him. Julia felt a moment's apprehension, as anyone might when confronted with a big dog known for its protective proclivities. "She's friendly," the owner called. "Never met a stranger, will roll over and let you rub her belly if you're so inclined. I just like people to have the opportunity to see her straight off. If you're not a dog person, I'll put her away."

"No need for that," Julia said.

The man gave the dog a signal, and she lay down obediently, staying put while he walked forward with a hand outstretched. He was tanned and attractive with silver hair and keen green eyes. Julia would put his age at midsixties, perhaps. "Steven Marris. My dad's name is also Steven, but he's been Steve all his life. I'm either Stevie or Steven." He grinned. "Guess which one I prefer now that I'm not five?"

Meredith and Julia shook his hand.

"Ready to meet Maria?" he asked.

"Sure," Julia said.

He turned and called. "Ree, come."

The dog leaped to her feet and sped along the pathway. Julia had one moment to wonder if this was such a good idea, and in the next, the dog flung herself to the ground in front of them, rolled over and exposed her belly, wriggling back and forth ecstatically.

Meredith and Julia laughed.

"What a silly girl," Julia said, kneeling to stroke the smooth belly. The dog stilled.

"She'll lay there all day if you keep that up." Steven grinned. "Okay, Maria. Let's go."

As Julia stood, the dog rolled over and rose. She shook herself thoroughly from her nose to the stub of her tail, and then came up beside Julia and leaned.

"Whoa!" Julia braced herself, laying her hand on the broad head. "How much does she weigh?"

"About a hundred ten on her slim days," Steven said.

"One ten." Meredith looked at Julia. "I weighed that in high school."

"We both did," Julia reminded her. They chuckled.

"She's wonderful," Meredith said to Steven. "Thank you for letting us get acquainted."

"Sure thing. Why don't y'all come in and meet Daddy now? I told him he was getting visitors this afternoon, and he's been driving me crazy waiting."

"How old is your father?" Meredith asked as they entered through a big front door into a cool and spacious foyer. A slim, pencil-style Christmas tree decorated in all silver and gold stood in a corner where a wide staircase curved up to a balcony.

"He'll be ninety-two in February," Steven said.

Julia felt a tingle of excitement. Steve Marris was in the right age bracket to have known about the Denton siblings.

Steven led them through the house to a bright sunroom where an older man sat in a rocking chair with a crocheted afghan over his lap. A fireplace along one wall displayed three beautiful cross-stitched stockings bearing the names Steven, Lila, and Daddy across their tops. "Daddy, these are the ladies I told you were coming to visit. Mrs. Bellefontaine and Mrs. Foley. I told them to call you Steve."

"Please call us Meredith and Julia," Meredith said, indicating each of them. "Thank you for speaking with us, Steve. I understand you've lived around here all your life."

The elderly man nodded. "'Cept for when I was in the service. I was born in a house on this land, but it's been gone for a while now."

"Did you serve in the Second World War?"

Steve shook his head. "Just missed it. I was stationed in Germany after the war." He sighed. "What a mess the Nazis made in Europe."

"Don't get him started," Steven cautioned with a smile. "Can I get you some sweet tea or coffee?"

Both women accepted sweet tea, and the younger Marris went into the kitchen.

"So you were born a bit before the Great Depression," Meredith said. "I imagine things were very different then."

The older man nodded. "Yes, indeedy. We walked to school and helped with chores morning and night." He waxed eloquent about his childhood as his son brought in two tall glasses of tea with mint and set them on soapstone coasters before each of the partners. "I don't remember them as being so bad, since that was all we knew. And truth to tell, we were in pretty good shape compared to a lot. My family had a little farm, so we were able to put food on our table and help out some other folks who weren't as lucky. But those were hard times."

"I imagine a lot of families struggled to survive," Meredith said.

"Some didn't survive," he said soberly. "Some couldn't make ends meet and just up and left from one day to the next. My folks knew of a couple of people who killed themselves, times were so tough. I was just a kid, but you hear the grown-ups talking, and that kind of story sticks with you."

"Steve," Julia said, "we are hoping to find some information about a little girl who was sold or adopted here in the area when you were young. Do you remember anything about that?"

Steve Marris harrumphed. He shook his head, and Julia's heart sank. "I don't remember any little girls getting sold," he said, "but there was a boy in my class who got sold to a local widow lady."

Julia gasped in surprise. This was not what she'd expected. But perhaps… "Do you remember his name?" She held her breath.

"Denton," Steve said without hesitation. "Sumner Denton."

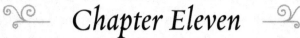

Chapter Eleven

"Sumner Denton?" Julia was thrilled. Perhaps in her wildest dreams she'd hoped he might have heard of the situation, but she certainly hadn't expected it to be this easy.

"Yes. He started going to school with me one day when I was pretty little—maybe first grade? Everyone said an old lady bought him to help with her chores, and maybe she did, but he was always dressed as decent as any of the rest of us, and she must've fed him well. He was one of the biggest and strongest kids in the school as we got older. One of the smartest too. I think he mighta been a year older'n me, but he'd never been to school so they stuck him in my grade. Yeah." He nodded. "First grade. That's when it was."

"What happened to his family?"

Steve shrugged. "I don't know. Not sure I ever knew." He made a wry face. "Little boys aren't nearly as curious about that kind of thing as they are how far you can spit or throw a ball."

Julia chuckled. "I imagine that's true. Did he have any brothers or sisters that you know of?"

Steve thought for a minute, squinting his eyes as he looked back over more than eight decades. "I don't think so. I never heard talk of any other kid that was bought, and I'm certain he didn't have any siblings in our school."

"Mr. Marris—Steve." Meredith sat forward, taking the lead. "How long was Sumner Denton in school with you?"

"Up until he quit," the elderly man responded promptly.

"Why did he quit?" That didn't make sense when Sumner Denton had just been described as one of the smartest of the classmates.

"He joined the army. He was older'n me, even though he was in my grade, but I'm pretty sure he lied about his age to enlist, because there's no way he was eighteen. I believe he must have joined in late '43, because I know he saw action in Europe. All us kids were jealous as heck. We thought that was pretty glamorous back then." He chuckled but quickly sobered. "Young kids think they're invincible. Doesn't seem so glamorous now."

"Steve?" Julia broke the momentary silence. "Did you ever see Sumner again after he went to war?"

Steve looked startled. "Of course I did. He came back here after his kids were grown. Betsy, his wife, was his nurse when he was wounded in the war over in Europe. They lived in Springfield, but our churches got together for fellowship suppers and the like, so my wife and I got to see them once in a while."

Julia could feel her heart beating faster. "Do you know if Sumner is still living?"

Steve frowned, and Julia's heart sank. Then he said, "Last I heard, he was. Do you know, Stevie?"

His son had been lounging against the doorframe listening to his father's reminiscences. "I believe so. His wife died a couple of years ago, and after that, he moved in with one of his grandkids, and they sold the old house where he'd lived."

Julia couldn't believe it. They hadn't even been hoping to find Sumner this way, and they'd literally stumbled over someone who knew him. "Do you have any way to contact him?" she asked. "We'd love to speak with him about that picture. We've tried to contact him, but all we had was a phone number. It's still connected, but it just rings and rings. We haven't even been able to leave a message."

"I don't know about that, but I can give you a phone number for his grandson," Steven told them. "We're both on the board of a local historical society."

"Wow," Meredith said. "Coming out here to chat with you two has been quite a help. Thank you so much."

"Anytime," Steven said. "Just do us a favor and let us know how this ends, if you ever find one of his siblings."

"Absolutely." Julia rose and offered her hand. "Again, we're deeply appreciative."

Ten minutes later, they were back in the car and headed toward the eatery in Guyton. They shared a moment of elation and then were quiet, trying to absorb what had just happened.

As they got out of the car in front of the same tired-looking diner where they'd met Sally Davis only a day earlier, they heard a "Yoo-hoo!" from several spaces away.

"Howdy," Sally called, moving toward them. "I've been waiting a while."

"Sorry," Julia said. "We got held up by something else."

"Did you bring the reward?" Sally was hard to miss in a caftan-style dress of an eye-popping green covered with orange and yellow flowers. It was quite long and flapped around her ankles as she walked, showing glimpses of velveteen-covered flip-flops.

"Did you bring your grandmother's paperwork?" Meredith countered.

Sally held up a thin legal-sized envelope. "Right here. Shall we trade?"

Julia raised an eyebrow and held out a hand. "What, exactly, is in this envelope?"

Sally immediately drew the envelope back. "Oh no, a trade's a trade. You gotta pay for this."

Meredith let out an unladylike bark of incredulous laughter. "You expect us to pay you for something we haven't even seen?"

"Yes," Sally said stubbornly.

"No," Julia countered. "Not a chance."

"Those papers could be useless," Meredith said.

"They could be real helpful," the woman said, calculation evident in her green eyes. "If you never see them, you'll never know."

"Tell us again where your grandmother was born?" Julia asked suddenly.

"Up near Athens—" Sally's face darkened. "You're trying to trick me!"

"I don't believe we're the ones playing tricks." Julia made up her mind. "We're not doing this," she said. She turned to Meredith. "Let's go."

Meredith nodded. "We have other leads to pursue."

The woman's round face flushed an unattractive deep red. "You'll be sorry," she said, shaking the envelope at them. "This here's puredee proof that my granny is that kid in the picture! And the price might go up if you don't want it today!" She whirled and stomped back to her car.

Meredith and Julia turned and climbed into Meredith's vehicle.

"Puredee proof," Julia said reflectively. "My grandfather used to say that. I haven't heard that in years."

"What does it even mean?" Meredith wondered, backing out of the space.

Julia swiped her phone screen and typed into the search engine. "Googled it," she announced a moment later. "'Early nineteenth century, southern slang,'" she read. "It means 'total, complete, the real deal.'"

"Oh dear," Meredith said mildly. "Now I feel even worse about missing out on puredee proof." She grinned.

Julia chuckled. "I'm fairly convinced that there is nothing worthwhile in that envelope. I'm not even a little worried that we made the wrong decision."

"Not after you got her to admit that her grandmother wasn't born here," Meredith said, grinning. She shook her head as she turned the car southeast toward Savannah. "There goes one lead I'm not sorry to see evaporate."

Back at the office, Meredith pulled into a space behind the building. "Oh, look. That's Chase's car! What on earth is he doing in Savannah on a Wednesday?"

Julia smiled. "He must be inside. Let's go find out."

Meredith rushed up the back steps and hurried inside. "Chase?"

"Hey." His voice came from down the hall, and as they headed toward their offices, he stepped out of Meredith's. He was wearing khakis and a polo shirt with a sweater draped over his shoulders in deference to the season, and his blond hair gleamed beneath the lights.

Carmen was nowhere to be seen, although Julia heard her call, "Hello. Any luck today?"

That was odd. Normally, if Meredith was out of the office when Chase stopped by, he would lounge by Carmen, teasing and making small talk until Meredith showed up.

Meredith veered toward Chase, while Julia went toward the reception area to find Carmen. She was seated at her desk busily typing on her keyboard. Julia might have imagined it, but Carmen seemed to be attacking the keys with unusual energy. "Lots of email today but nothing important," she said without looking up. Then she stopped typing and shot Julia a smile and a questioning look. "So did you get any new information?"

"We did. How long has Chase been here?"

Carmen shrugged. "Ten minutes? I offered him coffee, but he wasn't interested, so I showed him into Meredith's office to wait for her." She looked back at her monitor, her expression closed.

Julia knew that mulish look. There was no point in saying anything else. "We didn't learn anything else about the girl in the picture, but we did find someone who knows Sumner Denton and gave us his son's phone number."

"What?" Carmen clapped her hands together. "That's exciting!"

Julia gave her the recap of their discussion with the father and son and threw in the conversation with Sally Davis for good measure. "So she finally tripped herself up and admitted that her grandmother wasn't born locally. But she was madder than a wet hen when we wouldn't give her any money."

Carmen laughed and shook her head. "What a piece of work." Then she made a shooing motion. "So are you going to call the number for Sumner Denton's son? I can't wait to hear if he's learned anything else in the years since that story was first published."

"I am." Julia made for the door. Chase was just coming out of Meredith's office. "Hey, you," she said to him. "What are you doing in town midweek?"

"Just helping out a friend," he said easily. "I thought I'd come by and say hello to Mom. I'm heading out now." He hesitated, looking at the reception desk as if he was thinking of approaching, but then he turned away. "I'll see you soon."

If Julia was a betting woman, she was pretty certain she'd win a bet that Carmen had been polite but frosty to Chase before they'd returned.

Julia walked past the coffee station and back along the hallway to her office, plunked her purse down, slipped her jacket off, and placed it on the back of her chair. She dug into her bag for the paper on which Steven Marris had written the phone number for her. She picked up the office phone, and dialed the number for Leo Denton, the grandson Sumner lived with.

No one answered her call, so Julia left a message. She gave her name and the agency's and asked Leo if she could speak to his grandfather about the article that had been rerun in the *Savannah Morning News.*

Julia left her telephone number and ended the call. As she did so, she realized a whole kaleidoscope of butterflies was flying around in her tummy. She pressed a hand to her middle. It was possible that in the intervening years since the article had come out, Sumner Denton had found his missing sibling, and there was nothing more for them to do. It would be nice to have answers to some of the little mystery, even if they never learned why Miss Cora's mother had saved the article in the first place.

Meredith knocked on Julia's doorframe. "Hey, can you look over the invoice for Gaye Strieter? If you're going to be seeing her soon, you can just take it along with you and give it to her."

Julia nodded. "I'm going to meet her shortly. I plan to lay it out for her. We're wasting our time and her money unless she has additional, specific information about her son-in-law's alleged cheating. Oh, hey"—she lowered her voice and beckoned Meredith farther into the room—"while you're here, let's talk about a certain receptionist's Christmas bonus. I don't want to forget."

"Good idea."

"Did you have any figure in mind?"

Just then, they both heard Carmen walking toward the office, her heels tapping on hard wood, then muffled by the carpet runner. "Meredith, you've got a phone call." She appeared in the doorway. "There you are."

Meredith grabbed a sticky note from Julia's desk and scribbled something on it. "Here's that information you asked me to provide," she said to Julia, handing her the note. Her back was turned to Carmen, and she sent Julia a mischievous wink.

Julia glanced at the note. On it was written a very generous bonus suggestion. She nodded at her partner with a brilliant smile before Meredith turned to follow Carmen back out of the office.

***

At the close of the workday, Julia reluctantly donned her jacket and picked up her things. She had made arrangements to meet

Gaye at the piano restaurant at the historic 17Hundred90 Inn on East President Street. The ambiance there was soothing and enjoyable. It was one of her favorite places in the whole town to dine. She hoped it would make the conversation less contentious.

She got lucky and found a space curbside only a block away from the large brick-and-frame building, part of which was over two hundred years old. Although she'd asked Gaye to meet her at five thirty, her former friend was already seated and waiting when she arrived ten minutes early. Their table was close to a large white-trimmed Christmas tree dripping with decorations and lights.

Gaye waved at her from across the room. She wore a taupe pantsuit and a patterned scarf in greens and browns that accented it nicely.

"You're an early bird," Julia said after exchanging conventional greetings and slipping into a seat across from Gaye.

"So are you. That's why I made sure I wasn't late. You used to hate that," Gaye said, laughing. "Remember?"

Julia almost said, "Not really," but she didn't want to flat-out lie, because she *did* remember. Fortunately, she was saved by a prompt server who swooped in to take their order. "Just sweet tea for me," she said.

Gaye looked disappointed. "Can't you stay for a meal?"

Julia shook her head. "I should get home as soon as we're done. Beau will be waiting."

Gaye gave her order, adding an appetizer of crab-stuffed mushrooms that she clearly hoped Julia would share.

"So," Julia said, "let me update you." She handed the envelope with a summary of their activities and an invoice across the table.

"We've watched your son-in-law, Oren Vance, at different hours for ten days now, and we've seen no sign that he's engaging in any illicit activities. Is it possible he's involved with someone online and not stepping out in person? You haven't been specific about what led you to believe he's conducting an extramarital affair. We can't help you without more information."

"I doubt he's spending time with anyone online. He barely uses the computer when he's not working. Ten days isn't really that long," Gaye began, but Julia didn't let her continue.

"I'm going to ask you some questions," Julia said, taking out a notepad and pen. "Answer to the best of your knowledge. You may not know, and if so, just say so. Has your daughter told you she thinks her husband is cheating?"

Gaye gasped. "Of course not!"

"Is he disrespectful to her, publicly or in private, that you know of?"

Gaye shook her head. "No."

"Has your daughter mentioned that their relationship is better than it used to be, or conversely, are they barely speaking?"

"I don't believe anything has changed." Gaye sounded subdued. "I—"

"Next," Julia forged ahead, "is he protective of his phone? Does he guard it or leave the room to answer a call or text?"

"Well, he gets calls from the hospital, so sometimes. But he's always done that."

"Any unexplained charges on his credit card? Has she found any odd receipts that make her suspicious—"

"Julia. Stop." There was a weary note of command in Gaye's voice.

Julia looked up from her list. "These things are important. There could be clues—"

"Oren's not cheating," Gaye said. "It was the only thing I could think of to get you to talk to me. And I've been feeling awful about it. He doesn't deserve to have you spying on him. He's a wonderful husband and father and a wonderful son-in-law. I love him like he's my own child." Tears welled in her eyes. "And I'm so ashamed of myself."

Julia was dumbfounded. Not knowing what to say, she said nothing.

Gaye fumbled in her purse, and Julia realized she was hunting a tissue. Silently, she opened her bag, extracted a travel pack, and handed it across the table.

"Thanks." Gaye pulled a tissue free and dabbed at her eyes. "You always were ridiculously prepared."

"And you were…not." Julia had to smile. Once she'd had to make good on a threat to leave without Gaye if she wasn't ready when Julia arrived to pick her up. It had helped marginally. From then on, Gaye had been a teeny bit closer to being ready. The memory warmed her in a way it wouldn't have just a week ago. Was it time to try to heal this old wound?

Gaye's lips curved, but the expression looked forlorn. "I don't need to take up any more of your time. Please apologize to Meredith for wasting her time as well as yours. I wanted so badly to mend what I ruined all those years ago, and I thought maybe if we just spent a little time together, we could find our old friendship." She handed the packet of tissues back, stuffed the used one into her bag, and slid her chair back. "I'll put a check in the mail tomorrow."

"Gaye." Julia held out a staying hand.

Her old friend froze.

"I don't think we can go back in time to the way things were," she said, and the small flare of hope in Gaye's eyes faded. "But," she continued, "we have a foundation to build on for a new relationship. I'm willing to try if you'll forgive me for being so unforgiving."

"Oh, Julia." Gaye pulled her chair back up to the table. "I've hated myself for years for the way I treated you. I—"

"We all do stupid things when we're young," Julia interrupted. "And sometimes it's so hard to figure out how to fix them that it's easier just to do nothing and let time pass."

"And then one day, you realize that your life is more than half over, and it soon could be too late." Gaye sighed. "It was easier when you were four hours away, and I could pretend you didn't exist anymore. But since you came back to Savannah, and especially since I saw you the Saturday of the House Tour, the way I treated you has preyed on my mind. I didn't want my life to end without being on good terms with you again."

Now it was Julia's turn to swallow hard. It was good to know their friendship had meant so much to Gaye that she'd risked rejection to reach out to fix it. "I've missed you," she confessed. "I didn't like to think about you at all."

"I'm so sorry I hurt you like that. So sorry I wasn't more mature and less led by the need to be part of the crowd. Did you know I didn't send any of my kids to UGA?" she asked. "I didn't like the person it turned me into. One daughter went to Bryn Mawr, one went to SCAD, and my son went into the army after West Point."

Julia laughed. "That's quite a variety."

"I just wanted them to follow their hearts." Gaye smiled. "You certainly followed yours. I can remember you talking about attending law school when we still were in high school. And now you're a retired judge, while I'm...a housewife with an expensive education." She made a wry face. "I should have been more ambitious, I guess."

"But mothering your children well and volunteering is important too," Julia said, "and from what I've seen, you're extremely effective in your chosen organizations."

"Thank you." Her old friend's face turned pink.

"Gaye?"

"Yes?"

"I may have fibbed about needing to get home. If you have time, let's get dinner."

"Oh! That would be wonderful." Gaye sounded on the verge of tears again.

Julia picked up her phone. "Just let me text Beau and tell him to feed himself."

Chapter Twelve

WHEN JULIA ARRIVED AT THE office on Thursday morning, Meredith was just getting out of her car. She waited while Julia parked, and they walked into the building together.

"I spoke with Kenny Swann again after you left yesterday," Meredith told her. "He would like us to meet at his office at ten this morning. He plans to have Hilly come in, and he'd like us to be there to present evidence, if needed."

Julia wrinkled her nose. "My least favorite part of the job. Why do we need to be involved?"

"We don't," Meredith said promptly. "But you heard what he said. He wants witnesses, and he'll pay us to be there. So why not?"

Julia laughed. "Trust you to put it in perspective."

Carmen greeted them at the back door. She was literally bouncing up and down. "Guess what I just got from the answering machine messages?"

"Good morning to you too," Julia said, chuckling.

Carmen's red-and-white polka-dotted flared skirt swished around her as she did a little cha-cha-cha. "Mr. Denton's grandson Leo returned your call."

"What? That was fast!" Julia was thrilled. "What did he say?"

"His grandfather has agreed to speak with you." Carmen's eyebrows rose. "It almost sounded like Leo had to talk him into it."

"Hmm. That's interesting. Did he say when?"

"Two o'clock this afternoon, if that works for you."

"Sure does," Meredith said. "We have an appointment at Swann Lawnscapes this morning, but the afternoon is free."

"And by the way, the Strieter case is now closed," Julia said. "Gaye doesn't need us to investigate her son-in-law anymore."

"Caught him in the act?" Carmen asked.

"No, just the opposite." Julia shrugged. "She says she was wrong and that she's confident he's not cheating."

"Oh." The phone rang, and Carmen dashed toward reception on red stilettos that made Julia's eyes widen. How on earth could she walk in those things, much less run?

Meredith was eyeing Julia with interest. "There's more to that story, isn't there?"

"A lot more," Julia admitted. "I'll tell you on the way to Sumner Denton."

"I'll hold you to that," Meredith said, before they separated and headed for their respective offices.

At nine thirty, they left for Swann Lawnscapes, located south-side on Montgomery Cross. Julia could see Lake Mayer sparkling in the sunlight as Meredith drove. She knew that a lot of different water birds overwintered there, and she wished for time to stop and walk the mile-and-a-half loop around the water's edge. Maybe she and Beau could do that over the weekend.

Swann Lawnscapes was only a few lights off the Truman. White lights had been strung throughout a great many of the balled trees on the lot, and Julia imagined that it was quite a sight at night.

They were ten minutes early. Meredith parked amid the trucks with the company logo and a number of employees' cars, and they sat for a few minutes. Julia told Meredith about her meeting with Gaye.

"You were right," she said. "I do feel better for having let go of that resentment and anger. It helps to remember just how young we were. And I'll admit, it also helps to know that it bothered Gaye all these years. If she'd brushed it off as no big deal, I would've struggled much more to forgive her."

"Maybe you should thank her," Meredith said with a twinkle in her eye. "After all, you said yourself that that experience made you more determined than ever to succeed and become the woman you are."

Julia snorted. "I'm not sure I'm *that* thankful," she said in a dry tone. She glanced at her watch. "Let's go in."

Kenny Swann came out of his office to greet them as soon as they walked into the modest reception area. Red poinsettias were stacked on a clever Christmas-tree shaped tier with a single white one at the top forming a star.

"Oh, I love that," Meredith said.

"Thank you," said the receptionist. "We sell them, if you're interested."

Kenny gestured for them to follow him. "Thanks for coming. Hilly should be here soon. Let's go into the conference room, and Mary Lee can send her in when she arrives."

"Is Mary Lee her replacement?"

"Yeah," said Kenny, grinning. "And she's terrific. Better than Hilly ever was. I hired her through a temp agency, but I'm going to offer her the job when the temp agency's contract is up."

Kenny led them along a short hallway and opened a door before standing back so the two women could precede him into the room. "I'll be glad to have this over and done with. Thank you again for everything you did."

"You're welcome." Meredith laid a folder on the table. Carmen had enlarged several images of Hilly walking around without her crutches, an activity that was certainly not in the limitations described in the official medical disability document that Dr. Tannen had signed.

She had barely finished speaking when the door opened and the receptionist said, "Okay to send Hilly back?"

"Absolutely." Kenny didn't rub his hands together, but Julia thought it was a close thing.

A moment later, Hilly Pettis appeared in the doorway, looking fragile and ungainly with her crutches. "Hey, Kenny." She looked a little surprised to see two women seated in the room. "Oh, hey."

"Hilly, this is Meredith Bellefontaine, and this is Julia Foley." Kenny did not name the agency or explain their involvement in the case.

"Hello." She smiled warmly, obviously in a very good mood, and Julia wondered why. "Are you the bankers?"

"Er, no," Julia said, confused.

"Hilly." Kenny drew the woman's attention back to himself. "Do you believe you're here for a payoff today? Or, more to the point, for an extortion?"

"Well, I'd rather call it a financial settlement," Hilly said. "A payoff or extortion sounds kind of ugly, doesn't it?"

"So does telling your employer that if he doesn't approve your disability payments you'll sue him," Kenny said coolly.

Hilly's cheeks flushed with rosy color. "I didn't mean that quite the way it sounded," she said apologetically. "It's just that I can't work with this injury, and if I can't contribute my share of our family income, we'll lose our house. I can't let that happen."

"Then I guess you'd better get a job," Kenny said. "Provided you can find one where you can sit on your fanny and do nothing all day."

Hilly flushed a deeper scarlet, but this time anger suffused her tone. "I guess I'll be seeing you in court. You can't deny a disability claim."

"Oh, I think I can," Kenny said. "I asked you here today to inform you that Swann Lawnscapes is denying your disability payments." He held up a finger when Hilly began to respond. "And here's why. These two women are private investigators. They own Magnolia Investigations, and they were kind enough to look into this case when I asked them. Meredith, may I?"

Kenny extended a hand, and Meredith placed the file in it. After flipping the cover back, he picked up the first photograph, one that showed Hilly tossing her crutches into the back of the white Honda. A second showed her standing beside the car at the bridal shop, crutches nowhere in sight, and a third showed her strolling into the store with her friend. "Additionally," Kenny said, "we know you and Dr. Tannen go way back.'"

"Clear back to the high school acting club," Julia elaborated.

"So I'd suggest, again, that you drop this claim."

Hilly's face was sullen. "I'll come back to work tomorrow. I need today to wrap up a couple of things and make arrangements for someone to pick up the kids from school."

Kenny looked incredulous. "Do you think I'd hire you back after this? Lady, you're going to have to talk someone else into giving you a job. I wouldn't hire you back if you were the last receptionist available in town. And don't think for a minute you can use me as a reference."

Hilly surged to her feet. "I think y'all are horrible people, spying on me like that. Private investigators." She all but spat the words. "Sneaks and spies is all y'all are." And before anyone could say another word, she stomped out of the room, slamming the door behind her.

Kenny looked apoplectic. "Blaming you for her own misconduct is abominable," he blurted indignantly.

Julia began to chuckle. "But look!" She pointed to where Hilly had been seated. "She forgot her crutches."

Kenny's anger abruptly dissipated, and a deep, rolling belly laugh escaped.

Meredith smiled. "She certainly didn't like knowing that she'd been caught flat out doing wrong, did she?" she asked tranquilly.

"I think we're done here," Julia said. "Kenny, it's been a pleasure. I'm sorry we had to meet under these circumstances. If you ever need anything again, give us a call."

As they exited the building, Hilly's replacement called, "Have a nice day, y'all," after them.

Back in the car again, Julia began to laugh. "'Sneaks and spies,'" she quoted. "That takes a lot of nerve coming from someone who was happily cheating her boss *and* the disability system."

"Can you believe her?" Meredith asked, as she drove past the lake back toward the agency. "She completely ignored her own responsibility and decided we were the bad guys!"

Meredith's cell phone rang. The car's speaker system showed that the caller was Maggie Lu. "I'd better answer that," she said, touching the button on the steering wheel to accept the call.

"Hey, lady," she said. "How are you?"

"I am absolutely wonderful and completely fantastic!" Maggie Lu's voice rose with excitement. "I became a great-grandmother last night just before midnight."

"Oh, Maggie Lu, congratulations!" Meredith said. "Julia's here with me, so that saves you a call."

"We're both thrilled for you," Julia added. "Boy or girl?" Unlike many modern couples, Clarissa and her husband, Philip, had decided to wait and be surprised when their child was born.

"It's a boy," Maggie Lu told them. "They named him Jacob Philip, for his great-uncle and his daddy. They're calling him Jake." Her voice wobbled with emotion at the end. Her son Jacob had been killed in action nearly thirty years ago during Operation Desert Storm. "My Jacob would be over the moon to have his great-nephew named for him."

"I bet Charlene's so happy to have a grandchild," Meredith said.

"She's lit up like a Christmas tree," Maggie Lu said. "Clarissa's water broke at home last night, and off they went. She labored for quite a while, and ended up having to have a C-section, so she's going to be in the hospital for a couple of days longer. The baby was seven pounds, fifteen ounces, and twenty inches."

"That's lovely," Meredith said. "We're tickled for all of you."

"When are you going to get to see him?" Julia asked.

"I'm going to the hospital this afternoon," Maggie Lu said. "I can hardly wait to get my hands on that baby."

"You give that little boy a snuggle for us," Julia instructed. "And tell Clarissa we'll be by to meet Master Jake the very first chance we get. Congratulations again, Great-grandma!"

As they said goodbye and Meredith disconnected the call, Julia said, "Let's stop at Punch and Judy. Habersham Village isn't all that far out of the way. I'll just get off on De Renne, and we'll wiggle our way over from there."

"Ooh, great idea!" Meredith said. Punch and Judy was a family-owned boutique specializing in children's things, especially baby and toddler clothing and nursery furnishings. Julia dropped by there often for baby gifts. It was a fun shop to frequent.

Minutes later, Meredith parked in one of the angled spaces in front of the shops along Habersham Street, and they headed into the store.

"I don't even know where to look first!" Meredith said, eyeing a display of dog-themed books paired with a variety of plush stuffed dogs that matched the dogs in the books.

Julia had barely gotten through the door when she was struck by a display of Christmas clothes and gifts. She got no farther.

Meredith browsed for a few minutes. "Oh, look at this," she called to Julia. "This is it!" She'd found a light blue hand-knit hooded sweater and matching trousers, and she also picked up a silicone teether that the shop owner assured her was the very latest and greatest in baby teething items.

Julia lingered by the Christmas display. After what Meredith laughingly called a ridiculous amount of deliberation, she finally chose a red-and-white plaid romper with reindeer wearing Santa hats embroidered across the chest, and an heirloom-quality version of Clement C. Moore's classic, *The Night Before Christmas*.

"Can we get them wrapped?" she asked the saleswoman.

"Absolutely," the woman said. She completed Meredith's purchase first and then Julia's, after which she carefully wrapped the gifts and tied them with shining ribbons before ushering them out the door.

Meredith's phone rang again as she drove up Bull Street on their way back to the Historic District from Midtown. "That's Carter," she said, glancing at the display before punching the hands-free button. "Hi, honey. Julia and I are in the car on the way back to the office. What's up?"

"Hi, Mom. Um, you know how I told you the kids couldn't go to the *Nutcracker*?"

"Yes?" Meredith arched her eyebrows, although her son couldn't see her.

"I don't suppose you still have those tickets," Carter said tentatively.

"I do," Meredith said. "Why?"

"Oh good," Carter said, relief evident in his tone. "Sherri Lynn told her family we couldn't get together that day because the kids already have plans with you."

"She—what?" Meredith looked as surprised as she sounded. "What did they say?"

Carter chuckled. "Let's just say there was some initial resistance, but when she put her foot down, it disappeared. I think they were too shocked to argue."

"I'm sure they were." Meredith glanced over at Julia and mouthed, "Wow!"

Julia mimed clapping her hands and gave her friend a thumbs-up. Meredith had handled her disappointment well, but Julia was delighted that she was going to be able to share the special tradition with her grandchildren after all.

After lunch, Julia and Meredith once again headed northwest out of Savannah to the area where Sumner Denton and his siblings had been born. This time, the house was a sprawling ranch-style brick home with fencing around adjacent paddocks and a barn at a respectable distance behind the house. Three horses grazed in a nearby field.

The driveway wound in a circle in front of the house. Julia parked, and the partners walked up the wide, shallow steps of the porch. Meredith rang the doorbell, and immediately they heard the deep, clear peal of chimes. Moments later, someone came running toward the door.

The heavy door swung open to reveal a boy of roughly Meredith's grandson's age, Julia decided, somewhere around eleven or twelve. He was a towhead, and although his hair was cut short, it stuck out in all directions, giving the impression of untidiness. Keen, dark blue eyes crinkled. "You're Great-granddaddy's investigator ladies, aren't you? I'm Mason."

"Hello, Mason, it's nice to meet you." Julia offered her hand and was amused when it was pumped enthusiastically as she introduced herself and Meredith, who suffered through the same vigorous greeting. "Are you out of school already?" she couldn't resist asking. "Has Christmas break started?"

Mason shook his head. "No. I had to go to the dentist, and Daddy said I could stay home the rest of the afternoon."

A man came striding into view. "Invite them in, Mason," he instructed with a tolerant grin.

"Come on in." The boy stepped back with a grand gesture indicating that they should enter the spacious foyer.

The man, handsome and tall with silver just beginning to frost his temples, said, "I'm Leo Denton. This is my son, Mason."

"I interviewed Great-granddaddy for a school project," Mason blurted. "He told me all about his life. He's a pretty interesting guy."

"We think so too," Meredith told him gravely. "We'd like to talk with him about his life."

Leo gestured toward a sitting room visible through a set of french doors to the left. "Why don't y'all have a seat, and I'll tell my grandfather you're here."

Mason threw open the french doors. "Come on in here and sit down."

Julia looked around the room. In one corner was a baby grand piano, and adjacent to it was a stand holding a trombone. Two other instrument cases stood nearby. "Someone here likes music."

"Me," Mason said. "Actually, my whole family does. Mom and Great-granddaddy play the piano, and I take lessons. Great-granddaddy plays trumpet and piano, and Daddy plays trombone, and I'm learning saxophone too."

"Where did your great-grandfather learn to play instruments?" Meredith asked.

Julia was wondering the same thing. Sumner's childhood hadn't exactly been the picture of normalcy.

"Mrs. Healy, the woman who took me in after my father died, taught me the piano. I learned the bugle in the army, and then the trumpet was easy after that." The voice was deep and gravelly. Looking up, Julia saw an elderly man, surprisingly tall and standing erect, in the doorway. She realized immediately who his grandson had gotten his looks from, as well as the boy who showed the promise of growing into a striking man. She walked toward him with her hand extended, introduced herself and then Meredith, who also rose and shook his hand.

He can't be in his nineties, was Julia's first thought, closely followed by, *The woman who bought him gave him piano lessons?*

"Thank you for seeing us, Mr. Denton," she said.

"So you got interested in that old picture," he said. "How'd you come across it?"

Julia hesitated. "Actually, someone found it in an old family Bible and gave it to us," she said carefully.

But Denton didn't seem to realize the significance of the statement. "Huh," he said. "Well, come sit down, and I'll tell you what I can." He gestured toward his great-grandson. "A lot of interest in my childhood around here all of a sudden. That one interviewed me for a school project a few months ago."

"I already told them. Wanna read it?" Mason piped up.

"We'd love to," Meredith said. "If your great-grandfather wouldn't mind."

The older man waved a hand. "Good idea. Might save me a lot of talking."

Mason gave a whoop. "I have some extra copies." He sprinted from the room.

Sumner laughed. "He's a pistol. Reminds me of myself at that age."

"I have a ten-year-old grandson," Meredith said. "He looks about the same age."

"He'll be twelve next month," Sumner said.

"How long have you lived with your grandson?" Julia asked. "It seems to me that having a youngster like Mason around would keep you sharp."

"He doesn't miss much, and he keeps me on my toes," Sumner admitted. "I moved here about four years ago. My wife passed, and then I fell and broke a hip and had to be in a nursing home for a bit, and after that, the family didn't want me living alone. Leo's father— another Mason, named for my daddy—and his wife moved to Florida, and my daughter lives in Atlanta, but I didn't want to move away from here. Spent my whole life in these parts except for my time in the army."

Julia did a rapid calculation. "You'd have been a little too young to have served in World War II, right?"

Sumner gave her a smile that could only be termed mischievous. "I fudged my age a bit to get in. I was almost sixteen."

Meredith gasped. "You were a baby! I can't believe they let you enlist."

Sumner chuckled. "I was big and strong and healthy, and they needed new recruits. It was late 1943, and we were gearing up for some big offensives. They might not have been as particular as they'd have been some other time."

"Here they are!" Mason rushed back into the room, out of breath and waving a sheaf of papers. He gave a set to Julia and another to Meredith.

"Thanks," Sumner said to his great-grandson. "Now why don't you bring these ladies and me some sweet tea and cookies?"

"Okay." The boy rushed away again.

Sumner settled back in the reclining rocker he'd chosen. "Go ahead and read. It won't take you long."

Julia began reading. The report, stapled at the top, was nine typed pages. It had been an assignment for school, and Mason had been asked to "interview a senior citizen with an interesting life story." She suspected there hadn't been another report in the class with quite such fascinating subject matter.

As she read about the changes in Sumner's life, the breakup of his family, his new living situation with the woman who, through her actions, sounded as if she'd actually cared a great deal for the boy she'd "bought," and the tragic death of his baby sister, she bit down hard on her lower lip and blinked rapidly to stifle the tears that were trying to escape. She didn't dare look at Meredith, who she knew would be struggling with similar emotions.

It was impossible to imagine what the child and his siblings had suffered.

The Interview, Part 4

Interviewer: So by the end of the war you couldn't find the sister and brother you still knew, one sister had died, and one had disappeared completely. And the lady who'd taken you in had died too.

SD: Yep. That's it exactly.

Interviewer: That's terrible.

SD: It was, but you know, I was a young man, and I had to move forward with my life. I got married to a woman I loved for seventy years—

Interviewer: Nana Betsy.

SD: Yes. Nana Betsy. And we had two kids together. Your granddaddy Mason, and your great-aunt. And Mason had your daddy, and your daddy had you. You were named for your granddaddy and your great-great-granddaddy.

Interviewer: That's pretty cool!

SD: I think so too.

Interviewer: So how did you find Burdie and Bobbie Dee again? Because I know you did. I've seen pictures of the three of you together, and I know Aunt Bobbie still lives up near Macon.

SD: Smarty-pants. I'll tell you how. Nana Betsy and I raised our children in a bunch of places. We were sent to army posts all around the world. We lived in Japan first after the war and then in Kansas, California, Virginia, Germany, Missouri, and Italy. Some of them more than once. Finally when I retired we came back here to Guyton where I grew up. That was in 1968. Three years later, we went to visit friends in Macon, and we went to church with them. And that's how I found my sister Bobbie Dee.

Interviewer: What happened?

SD: It was the craziest thing. We walked into the church, and a greeter handed me a bulletin and said welcome. And I looked at her name tag and it said Roberta Warrick. And I never would have thought a single thing about it except just then somebody walked up and said, "Bobbie Dee, we're running out of programs. Can we have some of yours?" And she said, "Sure." And I took a good look, and I was sure it was her, and I said, "My sister's name was Bobbie Dee. I'm your brother Sumner." And then I thought she was going to faint, and Nana Betsy and I had to help her sit down on a chair. And she looked up at me and said, "You're really Sumner?" and when I said yes, she hollered out, "Praise the Lord!" And it turned out that she was still in touch with Burdie. The three of us got together for the first time a few weeks later.

Interviewer: *It was really lucky that you found your sister and brother again. Did you ever find your other sister?*

SD: I did, but it turned out she had made a life and didn't want any of us in it. So that was that.

Chapter Thirteen

WHEN JULIA FINISHED READING, SHE paused as she laid the papers in her lap. She swallowed hard and cleared her throat, marveling that the man before her had lived through such difficult experiences. "It sounds as if you were very fortunate to have been chosen to live with Mrs. Healy. How old was she at the time?"

"She was old enough to be my grandmother," Sumner said, "but I don't know for sure. She didn't have any children of her own, and her husband had died in a farming accident years earlier." Now it was his turn to clear his throat. "She saved me, that's for sure. I could have been bought by some farmer as a field hand, like my brother Burdie and sister Bobbie Dee were. She probably saved them too, truth to tell. She sent me over there every Sunday with food. I know for a fact they hid some of it to eat during the week."

"So they left the farm not long after you went into the army?" Meredith asked.

Sumner nodded. "Bobbie Dee ran off with a boy, like it says in that interview." He nodded at the papers in her lap. "He lived on the next farm over, and that's how they met. She was never allowed to go to school or even church, or anything like that, so as soon as she got old enough, she took off. And then my brother Burdie—Burdett, he couldn't take it there by himself, so he took off too."

"Where did he go?" Meredith asked, and Julia recalled that was the point at which Sumner had lost touch with both siblings for a while.

Sumner chuckled. "Only about ten miles over to Stilson. He got work with a construction crew. Stayed and worked for the same company till he retired."

"And you found him through your sister?"

Sumner nodded. "Bobbie Dee kept in touch with him. She married Austin Warrick, the feller she took off with—they're still married to this day—and they settled up near Macon, where I found her at her church. Not too long after that, she and Burdie and I got together for the first time." The old man fell silent for a moment. "Burdie and his wife never had any kids. He was a heavy smoker, and a couple of years after he retired, he had a heart attack. This year was thirty-one years since he died." He shook his head. "How can that be?"

Julia couldn't bear to touch on the death of his youngest sister Tillie, who'd died of pneumonia as a child.

"Did you make a career of the army?" Meredith stepped in, gently guiding the conversation in an easier direction.

Sumner nodded. "Twenty years. My wife was a British nurse. We met when I took some shrapnel in my left leg in the spring of '45, and we married right after the war. The army took us all over the world."

"What did you do once you got out of the army?"

Sumner smiled. "I started repairing furniture as a hobby. Started getting requests from people to repair their antiques. Sometimes I still get folks asking if I'll do some work for them, but I mostly refer them to my grandson. He learned from me, and he's gotten better'n I ever was." There was obvious pride in his voice.

"I'm gonna be a woodworker someday too," young Mason declared. Julia realized with a start he'd been listening with rapt attention to his great-grandfather's recollections. She wasn't sure it would be appropriate to speak of Cora Chisholm in the child's hearing.

"Ah, Sumner," Meredith said, to whom the same thought had evidently occurred, "we have a, well, a delicate matter to discuss with you."

"Mason," the old man said promptly. "Skedaddle. I'll let you know when you can come back."

"Aw, Great-grandaddy." The boy rose to his feet even as he protested. "I never get to hear the good stuff," he complained.

Julia chuckled as Mason left the room, feet dragging.

"So what's the deal?" Sumner asked. "I knew you didn't come all the way out here just to hear an old man reminisce."

"It's been quite fascinating, but you're right," Julia said. "When we arrived, we mentioned the photo that had been found in an old Bible. We were hired by the woman who found it. It was her mother's Bible. She's very anxious to understand why her mother would have kept that photo all these years."

"Sumner," Meredith said, "the sister you've never found—can you tell us her name?"

The warmth and levity had drained from the old veteran's face. "Corene was her given name," he said. "Why do you want to know?"

"I think there's a possibility, perhaps a slim one, that the woman who hired us could be your missing sister," Julia informed him.

"If her name's Cora Butler Chisholm, it's not a possibility, it's a fact." Sumner snapped out the words. "And I don't care to discuss it further."

"But—we—how did you know?" Meredith looked as poleaxed as Julia felt.

Sumner looked away. Then he inhaled deeply and sighed heavily. "Twenty-eight years ago, after that article ran in the Savannah paper, I had a conversation with a local lawyer's wife who recalled that her deceased husband handled two adoptions for the kids from the newspaper ad. She told me one of them was for my sister Tillie, and the other was for my sister Corie, whose real name was Corene." Sumner had just said he didn't care to discuss it, but he showed no inclination to stop talking. "I talked to the lawyer's grandson, who was also part of the firm, and he confirmed what his grandmother said. In fact, he still had copies of Corie's birth certificate and her adoption paperwork. He wasn't supposed to let me see them, but I guess he felt sorry for me, and he let me take a quick peek. That's how I found out the name of her adoptive parents. Mills and Lena Butler, a couple from up near Atlanta, adopted Corene and changed her name to Cora Butler.

"So I did some research on my own, and I found out that the Butler family moved back to Savannah, where their families were from, shortly after they adopted Cora. She was raised there, and she married Jasper Chisholm in 1950. They still lived in Savannah, so I decided I was going to go look her up." He snorted. "Worst idea I ever had."

"How old were you then?" Julia asked.

Sumner squinted and thought for a minute. "Sixty-five, I believe," he said, "and Corie would have been sixty-one. But when I went to the house, her daughter said her mama wasn't home and she spoke with me. At first I was delighted to meet my niece. I gave her my card and asked to speak to her mama. But when I told her my story, she accused me of being a charlatan who was only after her family money and said that couldn't possibly be true." His voice quivered with outrage. "I was a decorated army veteran, and here's this snotty society woman calling me a liar! I told her I wouldn't take a penny from them, that all I wanted was to find my little sister, and I turned and walked away." He seemed to deflate then, slumping in his chair. "A week later, I got a letter from a lawyer saying that if I uttered even a whisper about the Butler and Chisholm families, which came from a 'long and distinguished line of Savannahians,' they'd have me sued for slander. So then I figured she'd told her mother, and that was Corie's answer."

Julia felt as stricken as if the slight had occurred weeks ago, rather than nearly three decades.

"I told Bobbie Dee, and she said we ought to just forget about Corie. We couldn't change the past, and we had families of our own now. So I did." But it was plain that Sumner was still very bitter.

"I'm so sorry," Julia said. "We had no idea we'd be raking up such sad memories when we came out here to speak with you."

Sumner rose to his feet, slowly, and now he looked every one of his advanced years. "You'll have to excuse me," he said. "I'm very tired. I don't want to speak about this anymore." He raised his head and looked at each of them. "Ever."

Slowly, he left the room. Julia looked at Meredith, as shaken as she was certain her friend must feel. "This," she said, "is not how I expected this to end."

Leo came back into the room, a worried frown on his face. "My grandfather went to lie down," he said. "He asked me to show you out." His handsome features, so like his grandfather's, hardened. "I don't know what you said to upset him, but he looked like he aged a hundred years in the few minutes y'all spent alone in here. I'm going to have to ask you not to come back."

***

"Now what do we do?" Meredith asked as Julia drove back toward the city. "We might think we know that Cora Chisholm is Sumner Denton's sister, but we don't have a shred of evidence to prove it, other than his word."

"I don't know." Julia shook her head. "Cora Chisholm is roughly the same age as that little girl in the photo. I don't know her birthdate exactly, but it's got to be close."

"I've never heard a peep about her being adopted," Meredith objected. "This is a small town, all things considered. We'd have heard that if anyone knew about it, especially about a family that prominent. Adoption wasn't all that common back then, and in a small town like this, especially at that time, everybody would have known everybody else's business."

"She must not know she's adopted," Julia said. "Her parents never told her."

"Sumner said her daughter talked to him, not Cora herself," Meredith recalled. "If Cora doesn't know she's adopted, then the daughters probably don't either. Maybe she really did think he was some sort of scammer."

"It had to be Dolly," Julia said immediately. "She hasn't been happy about this right from the start."

"What if she went to her grandmother, and not her mother?" Meredith asked. "Cora's mother, Miss Lena, was still living then. Could she have been the one to sic that lawyer on Sumner?"

"Maybe, or maybe she didn't tell anyone and sicced the lawyer on him herself."

"But why would Cora's mother have kept that picture?" Meredith chewed her lip absently.

"If she didn't want Cora to discover she had siblings, assuming Sumner's story is true, it doesn't make any sense for her to have kept something so incriminating," Julia agreed.

"Who knows? Maybe she was sentimental and couldn't bear to part with that last shred of Cora's baby years."

"You said before that you wondered if her parents adopted her and passed her off as their own when they returned to Savannah. I think that's a very plausible theory."

"I believe Sumner," Meredith said. "I think what he believes is completely possible. But how do we prove he really is Cora's brother? We can't talk to him again." Her face fell. "We could kill him if we upset him too much."

Julia snapped her fingers. "The adoption papers. He said he talked to a lawyer who did the adoptions."

"It would be a lot easier on us if we could just ask him the name of the lawyer," Meredith said. "But I'm thinking we're not going to get that out of him now."

"I'm sure you're right about that," Julia agreed. "But that doesn't mean we can't find him ourselves. Good for us that lawyers never throw anything away. I bet those papers still exist. Or at the very least, they've been turned into digital files."

"If they do," Meredith said, "we might finally find out if Cora Butler Chisholm and Corene Denton are one and the same."

***

On Friday morning, the partners filled Carmen in on their visit to Sumner Denton and the details he'd added to the story. Julia had kept a copy of Mason's interview with his great-grandfather, and Carmen read through it with fascination, absorbing the additional details the partners provided.

"What we need now is a timeline," she declared when they'd told her everything they could remember.

"A timeline?" Meredith asked.

"Yes." Julia nodded. "We need to fill in everything we know about Corene Denton and Cora Chisholm. Let's see how many points of similarity we really have."

"We need to find out exactly how old Miss Cora is too," Meredith said, "and when her birthday is, although that may not be conclusive if adoptive parents changed it."

"Miss Cora said she's eighty-eight," Julia recalled.

"She did?"

"Remember? When she was talking about being a debutante," Julia reminded Meredith.

"Oh, you're right. She sure did." Meredith grabbed a yellow legal pad and wrote it down. So if she's eighty-eight now, she'd have been born in 1932."

"Corene Denton must have been born in '32 or '33," Julia asserted. "If she's the toddler pictured in that old photograph, which was taken in July of '35, she'd have been two-ish then, or maybe a young three. It's certainly not impossible."

Meredith continued to scribble. "And she said her family lived in Buckhead for the first couple of years of her life. But what if they didn't have her that whole time? What if she was adopted while they were up there, and they came back to Savannah sometime after July of 1935 with her, passing her off as their own?"

"Why July?"

"Because that photograph of the five children was taken in July, right before Sumner must have been sold, and I bet the others, especially the baby and the toddler, didn't take very long after that to place."

"Plausible. But we have to find a way to prove it."

"Those adoption papers are the key," Meredith said. "Carmen, would you start making some calls and check Google? We need to find out who might have been doing adoptions in Effingham County in the thirties."

"Steve Marris might have an idea," Julia said. "I can give him a call while you get started, Carmen."

Julia headed to her office and opened her planner, where she'd stashed the card the younger Marris, Steven, had given her when they'd visited on Wednesday.

"Marris residence, Nina speaking," said a woman when she called.

"Hello, this is Julia Foley. I visited on Wednesday, and I was wondering if I might speak to Steve."

"Steven the elder?"

"Yes, please."

"One moment while I see if Mr. Marris Senior is available," the woman said. There was a click, and the soothing tones of Pachelbel's Canon in D played. Julia realized she had literally been put on hold, something unusual for a private residence.

She had listened to the melody twice through when a male voice said, "Well, hello, Julia. It's Steve. You need more help?"

"I do," Julia said. "May I pick your brain for some old memories?"

"You can try," Steve said. "Don't know that there's much in there but cotton wool anymore."

"Ha. I know better than that." Julia was enjoying their banter. "I'd like to ask you about lawyers. Specifically, lawyers that might have been around when you were a kid, or even a young man. Anything you can remember might be helpful."

"Hmm. Let me think. There was only one lawyer here in Guyton that I can remember, and I believe there were two more in Springfield. Mighta been one in Rincon too, but I can't recall."

"Do you remember the names of the lawyers or their law firms?" Julia asked.

Steve chuckled. "The one here in Guyton is easy. Tidwell & Tidwell is the name. It's been the name since I was a child. I think they're on their fourth generation of Tidwells now. Over in Springfield, there was a firm called Dugger & Brinson, but I don't believe they're around anymore. And there was also a lawyer named Woods. Leroy Woods, Esquire. Don't know why I remember that, but I do."

Julia scribbled on a legal pad as Steve spoke. "Wow," she said. "You're a font of information. Cotton wool, indeed."

Steve laughed. "Have you tracked down Sumner Denton yet?"

"We did," Julia reported. "We had a chat with him yesterday. I really appreciate your assistance."

"Glad I could help," the older man said. "If you're ever able to tell me why you wanted to know about little girls being adopted and how that relates to my old friend Sumner, I'd like you to come back and visit again."

"That's a deal," Julia promised. "If I'm ever able to share it, I'll be happy to tell you the story. Thank you again for your help, and for these lawyers' names."

After ending the call she picked up her notes and walked up to reception to find Carmen. "I have some lawyers' names," she announced.

Carmen looked up from her monitor. "So do I. I just googled every lawyer in Effingham County and started calling. Some of them haven't been around long enough, but I found one, Dugger & Dugger, that said they go back to the early 1900s, but they used to be called—"

"Dugger & Brinson," Julia finished.

"Ah, you beat me to it!" Carmen shot her a mock glare. "Any others?"

Julia gave her the other two names.

"No Woods at all on my list," Carmen said, "but Tidwell & Tidwell is still around, except now it's Tidwell, Tidwell & Stone."

"Do you have contacts for either that one or Dugger & Dugger?" Julia asked.

Carmen nodded. She pulled a notepad from a drawer and wrote on it. "Here are the numbers of the firms. I only spoke to receptionists."

Meredith was on the phone, so Julia simply waved at her and returned to her own office, determined to get some answers.

Chapter Fourteen

FIRST, SHE CALLED DUGGER & Dugger. The receptionist put her through to someone named Wallace Dugger, who confirmed that the company had been founded in 1915 by a great-great-grandfather and a partner named Brinson who hadn't had any descendants to continue his name. But when she asked if the firm had ever handled adoptions, she got a firm no.

Next Julia called Tidwell, Tidwell & Stone. The receptionist there was a good deal more protective, and Julia had to mention investigating a long-ago adoption before the woman would let her speak to one of the partners.

"You'd better talk to Mr. Hardy Tidwell," she said. "He's the senior partner now, but the time period you're asking about would be from his grandfather's day. Hold for Mr. Tidwell, please."

A bare moment after she was placed on hold, a man with a pleasant tenor voice said, "Hardy Tidwell, how may I help you?"

Julia identified herself. "Mr. Tidwell, I'd like to ask—"

"You related to Beau Foley?" he interrupted.

Julia smiled. "He's my husband. Are you acquainted?"

"I've played a round of golf or two with him." Mr. Tidwell chuckled. "Please, call me Hardy. What I can for you this fine December day?"

"Well," Julia said, "I'm a private investigator, and my partner and I are looking for a little girl who was adopted out in your area in the early thirties. Did your firm do any private adoptions back then?"

"Oh, indeed we did," Hardy assured her. "My grandfather was the soul of discretion and did a number of them."

"If I gave you a name, would you be able to tell me if a child was adopted through your firm and who the birth and adoptive parents would be?"

"Might I ask why you want to know?" Hardy asked. "It's rather irregular to give out such information. Birth records are sealed in Georgia."

"I'm conducting an investigation for a client who may be an adoptee," Julia said. "She's nearing the end of her life, and her parents are gone. There's no one she can ask about her childhood."

"Hmm. Why don't you give me the name, and I'll see what I can do," Hardy said. "No promises now. I can't break the law, you know."

"I understand." But Julia still held out hope. "The little girl's birth name was Corene Denton." She spelled it for him. "And her adoptive name, I believe, is Cora Butler." She prayed Hardy would not associate the name with one of Savannah's society matrons.

"I'll be in touch," he said. "You tell Beau to hit 'em straight."

Julia laughed. "I will. Thank you, Hardy." As she hung up the phone, she realized she had crossed her fingers, and she laughed at herself.

Meredith popped her head into Julia's office midafternoon. "I'm taking off in a little bit. I've got to pick up my dress from the dry cleaner and wash this ratty hair before Quin comes to pick me up tonight."

"Oh!" Julia looked up from the files she was reading through. "I completely forgot the Penny's Place gala is tonight. I guess I'd better get out of here too. It starts at six, doesn't it? And that's a solid half-hour drive at the best of times."

"What are you wearing?"

Julia shrugged. "I have a dark green and a navy that haven't been worn for a while. Maybe the green, since it will be Christmasy."

"Long or short?"

"They're both floor-length. How about you?"

"I went shopping for a new dress the last time I was in Atlanta," Meredith said. "Everything I own has been worn a number of times. Plus, I'm in a little better shape than I used to be, so many of my things are too big."

"What'd you get?"

"It's a long burgundy gown with a wrap bodice and a sheer long-sleeve bolero jacket."

"Sounds very holiday-ish," Julia said approvingly. "Can't wait to see it." She shut down her computer and prepared to depart after Meredith left the building.

At home, Beau had already fed the brown tabby cat they'd acquired a few months before. Still, Bunny purred and wove around Julia's legs as she came in.

"Faker," Julia said. "I see an empty dish right over there. I know you've already been fed." She knelt and stroked the cat, who arched her back and made little chirping sounds. Finally, Julia rose and went to pick up the bowl and wash it before heading upstairs to get ready for the gala.

Beau was already half-dressed. He was seated at the desk in their bedroom in his tux pants and a pleated white shirt, looking at something on the computer. "Hi, honey." He swiveled his chair around as Julia walked over and kissed him. "How was your day?"

"Quite productive," Julia said. "I'll tell you about it on the drive, and you can tell me about yours."

Beau snorted and chuckled. "I played golf. That pretty much covers it."

Julia took a quick shower, then did her hair and makeup. She'd decided to wear the green, and after sliding on the deep hunter gown with its thin straps, she stepped into her favorite black satin pumps with a decorative crystal-encrusted square sparkling on the pointed toe. The heel was pencil-thin but only of moderate height, as she rarely bothered with truly astounding heels anymore. She'd had the shoes for years, and they were as comfortable as any dress shoe could get. A small black satin handbag with a thin black cord and a Christmas tree of sparkling crystals sewn onto one side came down from a box where she kept it for annual appearances, as did a loosely woven soft black cashmere shawl highlighted with thin sparkling strands in red, silver, and green that made it highly suitable for holiday events.

"Lookin' pretty fine," Beau drawled when she emerged from the en suite bathroom.

"You look pretty spiffy yourself," she replied. He'd finished dressing in the classic black tux he owned, paired with a bow tie in a black, red, and deep green plaid that complemented her dress. "Ready?"

"Ready," she affirmed.

Quin had offered to drive the four of them, and he and Meredith arrived minutes later, pulling into the driveway. Beau offered his arm to Julia to descend the porch steps and held the car door open while she tucked herself into the back seat.

Quin wore a black tux similar to Beau's. Meredith must have told him the color of her dress, because his bow tie was a deep burgundy that matched the fabric of her ensemble perfectly. As always, Julia was struck by how attractive he was, with his silver hair and twinkling eyes.

The two couples chatted, catching up on people they knew and recent local events as Quin drove, passing Lake Mayer and winding through some truly spectacular marshes. Then they crossed over Shipyard Creek and the Skidaway River.

"Oh, too bad the sun has set already," Julia exclaimed as they crossed a bridge. "This is one of the prettiest views anywhere in Savannah, I think."

"It is," Meredith agreed.

Passing the turnoff that led to Skidaway State Park, they continued into the heart of the exclusive private community, stopping at the gatehouse to show their invitation before they traveled farther into the island's premier enclave.

The Penny's Place gala was being held in the Grand Ballroom at the Plantation Club. Quin drove around to the gracious entrance that was lit by twinkling white lights draped over trees and landscaping. The men exited the car, helped the women out, and then Beau handed the keys to a smartly dressed valet. The front steps were wide and shallow with lit trees spaced at intervals on the broad front porch. Wreaths were hung on the front doors.

In the foyer, they picked up their table assignment cards and programs. Christmas decor was everywhere. An ice sculpture of a mother embracing a child, the Penny's Place logo, commanded the eye. It was situated between two Christmas trees decorated entirely in white, and there was a guest book on an angled podium beside a white poinsettia. They moved in that direction to sign their names before entering the ballroom, with its multiple bay windows and twinkling lights suspended from the ceiling.

As Meredith signed her name, Julia saw her freeze. "Jules!"

Julia stepped to her side, her gaze following the pen Meredith was using to point out a name near the top of the page: Dr. and Mrs. Andrew Tannen.

Julia gasped. "That's the guy who falsified Hilly Pettis's injury so she could collect workers' comp!" And Kenny Swann had decided not to report him, a decision Julia knew Meredith disagreed with as strongly as she did.

"Indeed it is." Meredith set the pen back in its holder with a smile for Quin. "And here you thought this evening was going to be fun and relaxing. Julia and I are going to have to fit in a little business, it seems."

Julia smiled. "We just have to gently convince one man that it is not acceptable to break the law, even on paper."

Beau watched, his gaze assessing both women as Julia signed for them. "You're not going to make a scene, are you?"

"Of course not!" Julia said, sincerely shocked.

"Southern ladies do not make scenes," Meredith said with mock severity, smiling at Beau and Quin. "We have far more effective methods of making our feelings known."

"I believe it," Quin said to Beau. "I feel sorry for this guy. I don't know what he did, but they're going to make him really, really sorry he did it."

They found their table. It was a large round table for eight, and two couples Julia knew casually were already seated there. People mixed and mingled during a predinner cocktail hour while servers set up four buffet stations for the meal to come.

"Should we find him now?" Julia whispered in Meredith's ear.

Meredith shook her head. "Let's allow the good doctor to enjoy his meal before we ruin his evening."

Meredith's former high school classmate Priscilla Fennell, who was chairing the evening, came bustling their way to welcome them, resplendent in sapphire blue chiffon with diamond and silver accents.

"Hello, darling," she said to Meredith, offering her air kisses to each cheek. "I'm acquainted with these other folks." She smiled at Julia, Beau, and Quin. "Welcome to our Penny's Place gala. I hope you'll consider supporting our work tonight."

"We certainly will," Quin said gallantly.

"Priscilla," Meredith said, "can you point out Dr. Tannen to me? I believe we have a mutual acquaintance, and I hoped to meet him."

"Of course." Priscilla scanned the room, then made a subtle gesture. "See the woman in the short red dress? Goodness, that's an interesting choice for an evening event at the Plantation Club. Anyway, the tall blond fellow beside her is Dr. Tannen. She's his wife."

"Remind me never to get on her bad side," Julia said, and they all laughed.

The meal soon followed. Priscilla gave a welcome, and then the attendees were free to move among the buffet stations, selecting choice entrée items such as juicy slices of rare roast beef au jus, citrus-glazed Scottish salmon, miniature crab cakes, and organic cakes of black-eyed peas and quinoa. Multitudes of side dishes were available as well.

After the meal, Priscilla spoke again about the work of Penny's Place, offering statistics laced with personal details about the important work they did assisting victims of domestic violence. Then she introduced a young woman, who stood and, in a surprisingly well-spoken and firm delivery, shared her personal story of escaping from domestic violence and the importance of supporting their work. "I was a helpless victim," the woman said, "battered, unable to leave my home, until one day I found the courage to make a choice to survive. And now I'm on the board of this incredible organization."

Julia found herself swallowing hard to maintain control, and to one side she saw Meredith discreetly wipe away a tear. Quin put a hand over hers and squeezed, and Julia saw that his eyes were shiny too. He was a good man.

The evening concluded with dancing.

Before Julia could nudge Beau to take her to the dance floor, though, Meredith grabbed her hand. "Look. Now's our chance."

Julia followed the direction of her gaze. Dr. Tannen's wife, she of the short red dress, had taken to the dance floor with someone else, and most of their table had followed suit. Dr. Tannen sat alone. "We'll be back," she said hastily to the men as Meredith pulled her to her feet.

The Tannens' table was on the far side of the dance floor. The partners skirted the tiled area where dancers were gathering, keeping to the thick, patterned carpet as they made their way around to where the man was seated.

"Dr. Tannen," Meredith said warmly as they approached.

The man looked up with no real enthusiasm, but he stood and smiled. "Ladies. Have we met? You'll have to forgive me—my mental files sometimes let me down."

"We haven't met," Julia assured him. "This is Meredith Bellefontaine, and I'm Julia Foley. We are private investigators, and we own a firm called Magnolia Investigations."

"How interesting," the doctor said.

"Kenny Swann certainly thought so," Meredith said. "Perhaps you know him? Swann Lawnscapes?"

Tannen had been about to take a drink, but his hand froze halfway to his mouth. Slowly, he lowered his glass. "I don't believe I do," he said.

"Oh, but I'm sure you know at least one of his employees," Meredith went on, wearing a razor-sharp smile that Julia rarely saw on her. "Hilly Pettis. I understand you were good pals back in the days when you both were in the high school thespian club. I believe you even acted in a play together."

"That's right." The doctor wasn't about to give himself away, Julia noted. "I do know Hilly. But I—"

"It's probably not wise to lie," Julia broke in. "Were you about to say you haven't seen her in years? Bad idea, Doctor. Because we know you've been in touch fairly recently."

"In fact," Meredith added, "we saw a document with your signature on it attesting to the fact that Hilly Pettis has an ankle injury."

"Don't put words in my mouth. I wasn't aware private investigators also had medical licenses," Tannen said. "What do you have to do with Hilly's leg injury?"

Julia opened her Christmas tree bag and pulled out her phone. She had never been more thankful for her habit of making digital copies of everything. After a moment of pulling up the proper image, she handed her phone to Andrew Tannen.

"If she's injured," she said, "it certainly didn't seem to be troubling her when this was taken a few days ago. And there are many more where this came from."

The doctor looked at the video of Hilly walking easily into the bridal shop with no crutches anywhere in sight. He was clearly surprised by the image.

"She told me she was having ankle trouble," he said in a low voice that betrayed shock and indignation. "I did an X-ray and didn't find anything, but she insisted she was having trouble walking. I thought it was possible. A lot of people have pain that's difficult to diagnose without a ton of expensive tests, and she said her deductibles were so high that she couldn't afford further testing. So I wrote her a note to be off for a week. I thought resting it would probably help."

"Wait." Julia blinked. "You wrote her a note? As in, physically wrote a note?"

"Well, we have a form," the doctor said, sounding puzzled. "I had my nurse print it out, and I signed it."

"So you did not sign a form for long-term disability?" Meredith asked.

The doctor looked even more taken aback. "No. Absolutely not. I couldn't certify any long-term issue. That would be illegal."

"Unfortunately," Meredith told him, "I think it's possible Hilly may have forged your signature once she had a sample of it. We saw it ourselves on a medical disability form she presented to her boss, who hired us to determine if Hilly really had an injury."

Dr. Tannen appeared stunned. After a moment of silence, he said, "I could lose my license over something like this. I would never falsify an important document like that. I thought maybe if she rested for a week, the pain would resolve itself. That wasn't unreasonable."

"No," Julia said, "it wasn't."

"So what do I do?" Tannen's voice held an appeal.

"That's up to you," Meredith told him. "We thought you had falsified information on purpose, and we wanted to..."

"Scare you straight, so to speak," Julia said. "But since you're another wronged party, as is Swann Lawnscapes, it's up to you what you want to do."

"I—I guess I need to speak to Swann Lawnscapes and tell them I did not authorize disability leave. And I guess I need to speak to Hilly." The doctor's voice hardened. "I'm not happy that she took advantage of an old friendship to do something like this. I'm not going to report her to the police—I don't have the heart for that— but I'm going to sever our professional relationship."

Chapter Fifteen

On Sunday afternoon, the last Sunday before Christmas, Meredith and Julia got together after their respective church services to visit the hospital and deliver their gifts to Maggie Lu's new great-grandson.

Julia parked in the parking garage beside Memorial Hospital, and they strolled along the curving walkway to the front doors. Inside, Julia's footsteps slowed as she saw an adorable display of baby items in the gift shop, but Meredith tugged her along. "No, no, no," she said, laughing. "We already have gifts, remember?"

Julia sighed. "But look at that giraffe. It's absolutely adorable."

"It's four feet tall," Meredith said. "Baby Jake does not need that giraffe."

"You're no fun," Julia grumbled with a grin as she followed Meredith to the elevator.

"I'm a great deal of fun," Meredith said loftily. "Quin told me he enjoyed the gala a great deal the other night."

"Nice!" Julia's interest immediately piqued. "Are you going to see him over the holidays?"

"Yes," Meredith said. "He's coming to church with me on Christmas Eve."

"Oh, lovely!" Julia was happy for her friend.

***

Monday morning, Julia was barely through the back door of the office when she heard a male voice coming from the kitchen.

"Are you going to tell me why you're giving me the cold shoulder all of a sudden?"

It was Chase, Julia realized, and since Meredith's car wasn't outside yet and Carmen's was, she had to assume he was speaking to their receptionist. She deliberately banged the back door to warn the pair that someone was entering.

"Good morning," she said as she walked past the kitchen door.

Carmen, in a full-skirted purple dress that was belted at her waist, was vigorously scrubbing a plate she must have just used. Chase, looking put together in navy trousers, a pink button-down shirt and a gray cardigan sweater, lounged beside her at the counter, arms folded and feet crossed at the ankle. He appeared very casual, but the tension in the room was thick enough to cut with a knife. The expression on Carmen's face made Julia glad that the younger woman didn't have any sharp implements handy.

"Good morning," the pair said in unison.

Julia kept moving, heading through the hallway to her office. Unfortunately, Chase made no effort to keep his voice down, and she could hear every word he spoke. She should have closed her door, Julia realized, but she didn't want to walk back across the room. The old house's floors transmitted every move.

"I'm not a mind reader," he said. "I thought we were...friends."

"Acquaintances," Carmen said firmly.

"Becoming friends," Chase shot back stubbornly. "So why, all of a sudden, do you avoid me whenever possible and speak as little as you can when you can't ignore me?"

"I have not been rude to you," Carmen said. "You are my employer's son. I will be respectful."

"But nothing more," Chase said, and there was mystified hurt in his voice. "Carmen, if you don't tell me what's wrong, I can't fix it. Won't you please—?"

A torrent of angry Spanish drowned out the rest of his sentence. In the tirade, Julia clearly heard the word *estúpido*. It didn't take a genius to figure out the English equivalent of that. Then Carmen switched to English. "I saw you at the Coastal Botanical Gardens light show with that woman. And then your mother showed off a picture of you with her again. You've been coming down here a whole lot lately, and your mother's barely seen you. What do you think you're doing, coming around here flirting with me while you're involved with someone else? I want nothing to do with you, do you hear? Nothing! *¡Por qué no vas!*"

"I know that means go," Chase said, "but I'm not leaving until we get a few facts straight."

"Get this fact," Carmen said. "I will not be one of a crowd."

"The only crowd you're in," Chase said in a withering tone, "is the one in your head. Will you let me explain?"

"Fine." Julia could almost see Carmen flipping a hand in the air. "Explain. And then go."

"The woman I was with at the light show has been a friend of mine since I was a little kid," Chase said. "And so has her husband. I was in their wedding. He's a commercial lender, and he's working on a really big deal in Texas right now. She's in the early stages of a pregnancy that's making her feel really terrible. They lost their first child about halfway through the pregnancy, and they're both really nervous about this one. He asked me to escort her to a couple of things when he couldn't be in town and to keep an eye on her. We're just friends, Carmen. Good friends." He suddenly sounded very weary. "And that's not something I can or will change. Ever."

Julia heard his footsteps leave the kitchen, and she lowered her head as he started up the hallway toward the front door. "See you, Aunt Julia," he said as he passed her door. "Have a good Christmas if I don't see you again."

"You too, honey," she said, but he was already past the door.

"Chase," Carmen called after him. Julia saw a purple blur as the young woman rushed past her doorway. "Wait."

The front door opened, but Julia didn't hear it close again. Chase must have decided not to walk out. Julia held her breath.

"I'm sorry," Carmen said. "I—er, I misinterpreted what I saw, and I apologize for hurting your feelings."

"It's not just that," Chase said in a low voice. "It's that you thought I was the kind of man who would do that sort of thing."

Carmen sighed. Julia could hear the sound from where she sat. It was impossible not to hear their conversation.

"I truly am sorry," Carmen said. "You know I grew up in foster care, *sí*?"

Chase must have nodded, because she went on.

"In several of the homes where I was placed, the men of the family, they—they preyed on young women. It's why I got moved from house to house so much. I kept a little canister of pepper spray on a chain around my neck. I had to threaten to use it several times. Once, I actually did have to spray it." Her voice shook. "I don't think you're like those men. I don't," she repeated. "But trust does not come easily to me."

"Carmen." Chase's voice was soft. "I'm sorry you had those experiences. I'm sorry you misinterpreted what you saw. In the future, will you just ask me if you ever have a question about my behavior? I'd really like to…resume our friendship."

"I'll do that," Carmen promised. "I would too."

At that moment, Julia heard Meredith coming in the back door. She sprinted to her doorway. "Meredith, I really need to speak to you," she said, grabbing her friend's hand.

Meredith looked mystified. "Okay, but I see Chase is here. Let me just go—"

"In a minute," Julia said firmly. "I need to speak to you first." She yanked Meredith into her office, closed the door, and leaned against it. "Those two," she whispered, "are clearing up a misunderstanding. They need another minute."

"Okay," Meredith said, her mind obviously moving on to something else. "Listen, while we're in here, I've been thinking…I think we should pay Tidwell, Tidwell & Stone a visit. If we wait until Tidwell Senior has had time to think about it, he may decide he can't help us."

"That's probably a good idea," Julia said. "We need to see that adoption certificate. It's the only way to definitively prove that Corie Denton and Cora Chisholm are the same person—if, indeed, that's what the papers say. It's possible we could be wrong."

"If we're wrong," Meredith said soberly, "then we may never find out why Miss Cora's mother was keeping a picture of the Denton children in her Bible."

***

Once again, the partners drove out to Effingham County.

"Might as well just put this car on autopilot," Julia said. "We've made a ridiculous number of trips out here in the past couple of weeks."

Meredith chuckled. "We have. And it's not like it's even a pretty drive."

She was right, Julia thought. It was flat, boring acre after boring acre of scrubby pine trees and sandy soil broken by fields. Fortunately, they were approaching the outskirts of Guyton, and according to the GPS, the law firm was just around a corner to the right.

Making the turn, Julia saw the sign for Tidwell, Tidwell & Stone above a well-preserved old brick building that had probably been standing since Guyton's heyday. A large plate-glass window bore the firm's name in elaborate gold script.

She parked along the street, and they climbed out of the car and entered the building. A receptionist sat at an elegant old wooden desk, but there was a modern computer setup with double monitors, and a printer with a fax machine sat on a credenza behind her.

The chairs for clients were leather, and a gorgeous old Persian rug in shades of pink and navy covered the floor. The place exuded luxurious charm.

"Good morning," chirped the receptionist, a round-faced woman with tight gray curls all over her head and the broadest smile Julia thought she'd ever seen. "How may I help you today? I didn't think any of the attorneys had appointments on their calendars this early."

"We don't have an appointment," Meredith said apologetically. "But we were hoping to speak with Mr. Hardy Tidwell if he's available."

"Junior or Senior?" the smiling lady asked.

"Senior," Meredith said. "My partner spoke with him on the phone on Friday. This is Julia Foley, and I'm Meredith Bellefontaine."

The woman rose to her feet. "Y'all have a seat for a minute, and I'll go see if Mr. Tidwell's in shape for visitors." She shook her head. "Sometimes that man has more papers spread all over his office than a wallpaper book."

Leaving the partners chuckling, she disappeared through a door that opened onto a hallway.

A few minutes later, she was back. "Mr. Tidwell says give him a few minutes to tidy up, and he'll be able to speak with you."

As promised, within five minutes, the door from the back opened. A short, dapper, silver-haired gentleman in a sharply tailored dark gray pinstriped suit came toward them, smiling as broadly as the receptionist. Julia was amused to note that he even had a small sprig of holly, complete with a cluster of red berries, tucked into his lapel buttonhole. "Ladies," he said, shaking hands first with Meredith and then Julia. "Hardy Tidwell the elder, at your service."

They introduced themselves, and the lawyer swept a hand toward the hallway. "Please, may I invite you into my office?"

Hardy held the door, and both women preceded him down the hallway, following his directions to a large office on the left at the very back of the building. It had large windows and was nicely appointed in shades of green and ivory. A small Christmas tree with a collection of red and black UGA decorations stood on an occasional table in one corner.

"What a lovely room," Meredith remarked.

"And so clean," Julia said. "Your receptionist led us to believe we might find you buried beneath a layer of briefs and research."

Hardy grinned. He walked to a credenza against one wall and opened the spacious doors on its front.

Julia was startled into laughing aloud as a ragged stack of papers was revealed, leaning precariously to one side. "Oh my goodness."

"Best piece of furniture I ever bought," he drawled proudly. "It hides all manner of indiscretions." He indicated chairs covered in forest-green leather and then propped himself casually against the front of his desk. "Now, ladies, how may I help you? I presume you're here about the matter of that adoption?"

Julia nodded. "We were really hoping you could help us confirm the identity of the adoptive child. We know what her birth name was, and we know who her adoptive parents were and what her name became, but we lack any corroborating documentation of those facts."

Hardy's face sobered. "I was able to locate the file, but there's something you must understand. Adult adoptees in Georgia do not have the right to obtain their original birth certificates or any information about the birth parent unless the birth parent has consented in writing to such disclosures. The only thing I am officially allowed to offer you is nonidentifying information."

"Twenty-eight years ago," Julia said, "a man named Sumner Denton came to your firm looking for information after your grandmother told him she remembered that your grandfather had done adoptions for Denton's sisters. He said the grandson, and I'm presuming that was you, confirmed it. We're not out to make trouble, Hardy. We have a client who may be the sister Sumner's been searching for, and we'd like to find that last link. She's eighty-eight years old, and Sumner is over ninety now. It would be nice to give them closure." She didn't mention that Sumner had found his sister. She didn't think that was her story to tell.

Hardy studied both of them for a moment. Then he turned and picked up a solitary file that had been left on one corner of his desk. He opened it, smoothed it flat, and laid it squarely in the center of his desk. Then he stood. "I can't tell you anything further about the case," he said, "except that in 1935, two little girls, one age nine months and one age two years and three months, were adopted through this agency to two different couples. One couple was from this area, one was from up above Atlanta. The surrendering mother had been widowed and consequently felt herself incapable of providing for the children. She did not leave any instructions permitting us to share information about the adoption at any time in the future, not even after her death, which, I understood from her son in 1992, was untimely and occurred relatively soon after these adoptions were completed." He turned and patted the file. "If you'll excuse me for a moment, I must go speak to my secretary." And with that, he winked and left the room.

Meredith looked at Julia, eyebrows raised in delighted shock. "Why, that sly old fox. I wonder if this is what he did for Sumner too."

"I don't know, but we need to look at that file quick!" Julia leaped to her feet, as did Meredith, and they rushed to the desk.

The file felt soft and worn with age, and the thin stack of papers was yellowed. They had clearly been typed on a manual typewriter.

The first was a Certificate of Birth from the State of Georgia, listing a female child born in 1932 in the city of Guyton in Effingham County to Mason Sumner Denton and Mildred Denton, nee Hanlin. The child's full name was Corene Helen Denton. Julia whipped out her phone and began to take pictures. Meredith did the same.

The second paper in the file was a death certificate for Mason Denton, who died in 1934. Cause of death was listed as a farming accident—traumatic injuries to the torso incompatible with sustaining life. She took a picture of that as well, shaking her head over the sadness of the young man who'd left behind a family of six with no means of support.

The third and fourth sets of papers were certificates of adoption, also issued in Georgia. Each was three pages long. Each listed the names of the birth parents and their address, the names of the adoptive parents and their address, and the name of the law firm that had handled the procedure. First they looked at Tillie's. Julia took photos of it in case Sumner or Cora would like to have a copy.

Then the partners turned their attention to the second set of adoption papers. The birth parents, of course, were Mason and Mildred Denton, and Mason was listed as deceased along with his date of death. The adoptive parents were Mills and Lena Dunwoody Butler of Buckhead, Georgia, and the child's new name was to be Cora Dunwoody Butler.

"Gotcha," Julia murmured, raising her phone again and carefully photographing each page. She glanced at Meredith, who was looking down at the paperwork. A tear ran down her cheek.

She wiped it away as Julia slipped her phone back into her purse. "These make it all seem so real," Meredith said. "What a tragedy for that family."

"It was," Julia agreed. She meticulously replaced the paperwork in its original position and closed the file.

The pair had barely resumed their seats when the door opened, and Hardy Tidwell returned. "As I said," he told them, as if the conversation had never been interrupted. "I am unable to tell you anything or give you the original certificate of adoption in this case, if indeed I have it. That would have been in my grandfather's time."

"We understand completely, Mr. Tidwell." Meredith rose, smiling serenely. "Thank you so much for your time."

"Yes, thank you." As Julia shook his hand on the way out the door, she gave it an extra squeeze, and his smile broadened.

"Y'all take care now," he said. "I hope the living family members are able to be reunited somehow."

"So do we," Julia said. "Thanks again for your time."

Back in the car, Meredith exhaled. "Well. Now we have proof positive that Cora is really Corene Denton. That's why her mother kept that photo all these years."

"Yes, but if she was keeping the photo for Cora, why on earth did she never tell her what it was?"

"Miss Cora's daughter has a lot to answer for," Meredith said darkly. "I wonder if Dolly went to her grandmother after Sumner's visit in 1992. Dolly would have been around forty at the time, if I'm calculating right, and she was probably panicked at the thought of the scandal that might develop."

Julia nodded. "She may have, and the grandmother, Miss Cora's mother, may have decided against telling her daughter about the adoption. Or maybe Dolly made the decision to turn Sumner away on her own. But the bottom line is, now we have proof, and we need to tell Miss Cora. No matter what Dolly thinks."

"Wait a minute, though," Meredith said. "What about Sumner? He's over and done with it, remember? He said he doesn't care if he ever meets her. He was really hurt by the reaction the last time he tried."

"Well, we have to convince him to try again," Julia said.

"I don't think so," Meredith said. "At least, not before we speak with Miss Cora. What if she's horrified by this? I don't want to get his hopes up, only to have them dashed again. I think we should tell Miss Cora first, gauge her reaction, and then contact Sumner *if* she reacts positively and wants to meet him."

Julia sighed. "You're right. Absolutely right. We can't speak to Sumner yet."

"Let's make an appointment to visit Miss Cora tomorrow," Meredith said. "We're taking Carmen out for our Christmas dinner this evening, and if we go this afternoon, we could get pressed for time."

Chapter Sixteen

THE PARTNERS HAD DECIDED THEY would have a special Christmas meal with Carmen at an exclusive local restaurant, Elizabeth on 37th. It wasn't usually crowded on a Monday evening, and they could leisurely enjoy their time together. They'd planned to close the office at three so they all could go home and relax, which Meredith said was code for taking a nap, freshening up, and changing into nice evening clothes suitable for a fancy restaurant.

Back at the office, Carmen met them the minute they came through the door. "What happened?" she asked. "I'm dying for details."

Meredith opened her mouth, but Julia said, "Wait." To Carmen, she said, "Before we tell you, will you please go call Miss Cora and make an appointment for us to visit around eleven tomorrow morning?"

Carmen gave her a quizzical look, but when Julia waited expectantly, she smiled and headed for her desk.

Meredith looked at Julia, brows raised. "What was that all about?"

Julia shrugged. "You can bet Miss Cora is going to ask her why we want to come by, if we've learned anything, that kind of thing. This way she can truthfully say she doesn't know."

Two minutes later, Carmen was back. "Okay, now can you tell me?" she asked, hovering in Julia's doorway.

"Gladly." Julia beckoned her in and gestured to the chairs by the fireplace, one of which Meredith was already occupying. Carmen sat down while Julia flipped through the photos on her phone to find those she'd just taken on their morning excursion to Guyton. "We struck pay dirt today."

***

The three women of Magnolia Investigations met that evening at six sharp at Elizabeth on 37th.

Julia and Meredith had agreed that they wanted to make it special for Carmen, so they'd talked up what they were going to wear, clueing their young employee in to the fact that this would be a dressy affair, even if it was just dinner. Julia chose a slim-fitting navy street-length dress. The bodice above the sweetheart neckline and long tight sleeves were made of lace. She had hauled a higher-than-usual pair of navy heels out of the back of her closet for the occasion, since she didn't have to walk far.

As she'd hoped, it didn't appear that Elizabeth's would be too crowded early on a Monday evening, and there was plenty of parking on both sides of 37th Street. She had just climbed out of her car when Meredith pulled into a space right behind her.

As her friend emerged from her car, Julia saw that Meredith wore a stylish deep red suit with a round velvet collar, velvet pocket flaps, and rhinestone buttons to give it sparkle.

"You look terrific," Julia said.

"So do you," Meredith replied. "We clean up pretty good for old ladies."

"Speak for yourself," Julia said, but she grinned. "Age is merely a state of mind."

"I believe that a lot more than I did a year ago," Meredith said. "You and this agency have been good for me."

They proceeded to Elizabeth on 37th. The restaurant was housed in a lovely, century-old cream-colored Victorian mansion. It was particularly lovely in the early evening darkness with strategic spotlights highlighting the fragrant herb gardens and shrubs along the brick walkway, the front porch, and the balcony directly above. It glowed with white Christmas lights strung around the porch, and there were large double wreaths on the front doors. The doorman, clad in smart black and white and wearing white gloves, opened the doors for them with a warm greeting, which they returned.

"Under what name is your reservation?" the concierge inquired.

"Bellefontaine," Meredith told him. "There will be three of us, and we'll wait here just a moment for our third, if you don't mind. I'm sure she won't be long."

Just then, the doorman opened the front door again, and a stunning woman stepped inside. Petite and shapely, she had a cloud of black hair that fell around her bare shoulders. Her black dress had a high neck with a modest keyhole detail at the bodice, but as she turned to shrug off the black shawl she wore, Julia saw that the back was open, showing off her flawless caramel skin.

"Carmen, you look fantastic," Julia exclaimed. The third member of their team wore more makeup than usual, but it had been carefully applied to highlight her high cheekbones, big dark eyes, and to-die-for full lips.

Carmen smiled. "You boss ladies look pretty fantastic yourselves."

They were shown past the large Christmas tree in the foyer to their table in one of the high-ceiling dining rooms. Waiters seated them at a carefully laid table and handed them menus.

Carmen's eyes sparkled with excitement. "This place is amazing! Are you sure it's not too expensive?" she whispered once they were alone.

Julia chuckled. "It's a wonderful dining experience for special occasions," she said. "And this, our first holiday together with Magnolia Investigations, certainly qualifies as special. As long as we keep it to once a year, it won't break the bank."

"Can I offer a prayer?" Meredith asked. The three women clasped hands, and Meredith uttered a brief but heartfelt blessing.

After Meredith finished, Carmen leaned to one side and picked up two small, shiny red bags tied with curling silver ribbon that she'd carried in. "These are for you." She set one in front of Julia and the other in front of Meredith.

"Oh, Carmen, you shouldn't have," Julia said.

"Don't get excited," Carmen said. "It's nothing special. You know I'm on a no-frills budget."

Both women had pulled open the bows on their bags.

Julia reached in and lifted out a small plant with bright red blooms in a pot sparkling with glitter and enhanced with a red bow. "It's a Christmas cactus!" she said. "Thank you, Carmen! I have one that blooms pink, and I've wanted a red one forever. What a perfect gift."

"It will always remind me of you," Meredith said. "I have the perfect place for it right above my sink. Thank you so much."

"Merry Christmas," Carmen said. "They came from my own plant. I know you realize how much this job, this opportunity you gave me, means. I only hope I'm doing a good enough job. If there's anything you need me to improve on, just let me know."

Meredith looked speechless.

Julia felt the same. "Oh, Carmen," she said. "You're so efficient you make me feel like a slacker. You keep us organized, you help with details, you often know what we need even before we do. How could you possibly think you're not doing a good enough job?"

Carmen gulped. "That's the nicest thing anyone's ever said to me, I think."

Meredith reached down to the purse she'd stashed beneath the table and pulled out two small tissue-wrapped squares tied with sparkly green ribbon. "Here's a little something for the two of you." She handed one to each of the others.

Julia untied her ribbon and tore open the paper, noticing as she did so that Carmen was carefully opening hers without tearing the paper. "You're one of those," she said, laughing. "A paper-saver. Hurry up, slowpoke!"

Together, they pulled out the small white cards hidden inside the paper. Attached to each was a pair of silver-and-enamel earrings. "These are beautiful!" Carmen said. "Magnolia blossoms for Magnolia Investigations. How perfect."

"Thank you," Julia said. "I love these. And now it's my turn." She presented Meredith and Carmen with her tokens, wrapped in silver paper with white ribbon.

It took them only moments to reveal elegant handmade rosewood pens, each engraved with MAGNOLIA INVESTIGATIONS, on the side.

"I love this," Carmen exclaimed. "Thank you, Julia."

"Yes, this is pretty special," Meredith said.

"I got one for myself too," Julia confessed. "I couldn't resist."

Meredith laughed. "And I may have picked up a pair of magnolia blossom earrings for myself as well." She paused and took a deep breath. "And now there's one last thing." She presented Carmen with an envelope. "Julia told you what a good job you're doing. We wanted to show you how much we value you."

Carmen's brows rose in question. She opened the envelope and pulled out a card. When she opened it, a check fluttered out and she caught it. Her mouth rounded into a silent O. As she read the words of thanks they had each written, tears filled her eyes. At last, she looked at the check, and she gasped. "Oh no!" she said. "This is too much. Much too much."

"No," Julia said, "it's not. We want you to understand what you mean to us, and to this business. We want you to be able to buy a car without it breaking your budget. And so, in addition to this gift, we've decided to raise your salary."

Meredith told her the new figure.

Carmen promptly burst into tears.

Meredith snatched a tissue out of her bag and offered it to Carmen.

"Without you," Julia said, "Magnolia Investigations would not be what it is—what *we* are—today. We did this because you're worth it, not because we felt sorry for you or any other reason." She held out a hand to each of her friends. Meredith did the same, and they linked hands around the table.

"You're worth it," Meredith repeated.

"I'm worth it," Carmen whispered, her eyes still shining with tears. "It's easy to believe that when I have you two to remind me."

***

Tuesday morning, Meredith and Julia stood in the front entry of Magnolia Investigations, bracing themselves for the coming meeting with Miss Cora.

"Ready?" Meredith asked.

"Ready as I'll ever be," Julia responded. "I wish I had a crystal ball to tell us how this is going to go."

"Good luck," Carmen sang out from her desk in the reception area. "I can't wait to hear what happens."

The partners left the office by the front door, crossed Whitaker Street, and walked into Forsyth Park. Six sidewalks radiated out from the central plaza around the fountain-like spokes on a wheel. They took one of those, walking diagonally to the fountain and around it to the path on the opposite side. It was a chilly but sunny day, and Julia was comfortable in a deep teal pea coat over dark charcoal trousers and a pale teal sweater.

At the corner they turned right and walked along the same shaded sidewalk they'd followed a number of times this month. The entire walk, from their door to the front steps of Devender-Chisholm House, took less than ten minutes.

Their first hint that things weren't going to be quite as low-key as they'd hoped occurred when they rang the bell. A familiar yapping preceded the arrival of the same small gray poodle who'd greeted them before.

"Oh great," Meredith said morosely. "That's Shelby's dog."

"Lancelot," Julia reminded her. "And his presence probably means that Miss Cora invited both Dolly and Shelby here today. I never thought to tell her we'd prefer to speak to her alone."

Meredith sighed. "Well, there's nothing to be done now. We'll have to go ahead as planned."

As before, Shelby Nichols scooped up her poodle and opened the door. She was clad in winter white, and she greeted them warmly before leading them to the same room where they'd visited with Miss Cora before.

Dolly was there, as was the housekeeper, Susan, who smiled and offered them hot tea or hot chocolate. Shelby perched beside her sister on a love seat after gesturing to Meredith and Julia to be seated.

"Just a glass of water, please," Julia told Susan, and Meredith echoed the request.

"Good morning, girls," Miss Cora said. "Do you have news for me?"

"We do," Julia said. "Miss Cora, we've spent the past few weeks trying to find some reason your mama would have kept a photo of five children from Guyton in her Bible, and now we know."

"We'd like to tell you the story of the family first," Meredith said. "In 1934, a man was killed in a farming accident out in Effingham. His name was Mason Denton…." Carefully, she described each development in the life of the family members—the mother's inability to care for them, the selling or adoption of the children, Sumner going to a widow who educated and cared for him, Bobbie Dee and

Burdie going to a farm to provide free labor, baby Tillie being adopted by a local couple, the mother's death by drowning....

"And the final one of the five was a toddler, born in 1932," Julia said. "Her name was Corene, but her family called her Corie."

Shelby put a hand to her bosom and took a deep breath. "Perhaps... perhaps, Susan, you should give us a moment's privacy right now?"

"Oh, don't be a goose, Shelby," Miss Cora said. "First of all, Susan's smart enough to know what's afoot after the beginning of this story, and second, she's family to me. I have nothing to hide from her."

Shelby cleared her throat. "Sorry, Mama. Sorry, Susan."

Miss Cora was sitting with her hands clasped together. "Now," she said, "please continue, girls."

"Miss Cora," Julia said, "Corene Denton was adopted by your parents, Mills and Lena Chisholm, who lived up in Buckhead at that time, and she was renamed Cora. You were born Corene Denton and adopted before you were three years old. Shortly after the adoption, your parents returned to Savannah, where their families were."

"Oh, Mama," Dolly said. She put both hands to her face.

Shelby appeared to be a stone statue. Her face had gone white.

Miss Cora shook her head slowly. Wonderingly. "I was adopted," she repeated.

"You were," Meredith confirmed.

"I suppose you have proof of this," Dolly said.

"A law firm in Guyton still has her birth certificate and the adoption papers," Julia said carefully. It was probably best not to mention how they knew that unless they had to.

Miss Cora fell silent. Finally, she said, "So I'm not actually a Butler."

"Of course you are, Mama," Dolly said sharply. "Adoption will never change that."

Silence blanketed the room again. Even the poodle had gone still.

"I suppose they're all gone now," Miss Cora said wistfully.

"No, ma'am," Meredith said. "Two of them are still living. Sumner, the oldest son, still lives in Guyton, and Bobbie Dee, the eldest sister, lives in Macon."

Miss Cora didn't speak for a moment. She reached for the cup of tea on the table beside her, but her hand was shaking so badly Susan came to her side and held the teacup so the older lady could take a sip and then sat beside her, holding her hand. Neither of the daughters spoke. Shelby still seemed frozen in shock. Dolly had silent tears slipping down her cheeks.

Finally, Miss Cora said, "I would like to meet my brother and sister. Do they know I'm alive?"

"Yes, ma'am, they do," Meredith said.

Julia took a deep breath. "They've known who you are for twenty-eight years," she said. "In 1992, Sumner found out your adoptive name and ultimately learned your married name and that you lived in Savannah. He came here to meet you."

"What?" Miss Cora cried. "But why didn't he? I never knew a thing about this." For the first time, she seemed upset.

"He did come here, to this house," Meredith told her. "But he was turned away without speaking to you."

"Turned away? By whom?" Miss Cora's voice quavered.

Julia looked at Dolly, eyebrows raised, but the elder daughter was watching her mother and missed the silent cue to speak up.

Shelby, who'd been quiet since they'd broken the news, stirred. "Oh, Mama, come on. This story has holes bigger than swiss cheese. They haven't shown you a copy of the adoption papers, have they? I bet this man is probably just a charlatan after Daddy's money."

Chapter Seventeen

SHELBY'S WORDS RICOCHETED AROUND THE room. Miss Cora didn't speak, but Meredith turned to Julia, realization and horror dawning in her eyes.

A loud alarm bell rang in Julia's head. As clearly as if he was standing in the room, she could hear Sumner's voice. *"She accused me of being a charlatan who was only after her family money...."*

They had suspected the wrong daughter. It hadn't been Dolly who'd turned away her own uncle—it had been Shelby!

Charlatan wasn't a word one heard every day. Or even every year, for that matter, but now they'd heard it twice within a week.

"You met your uncle twenty-eight years ago," Julia said, "and you turned him away without ever telling your mother. You used that exact word, *charlatan*. He remembers it to this day."

Shelby looked both stricken and defiant.

"Oh, Shelby," Dolly said in a thin voice. "What have you done?"

"It was the right thing to do," Shelby retorted, although her voice broke. Her face had grown red. She wrapped her arms around herself as if trying to find comfort. "I didn't want Mama to know, and I believe Grandmama didn't either, or she and Granddaddy would have told her a long time ago. After she died, I found a copy of that picture with a copy of Mama's adoption certificate, and I got rid of them. Grandmama would have wanted me to," she said urgently. She began to cry. "I had no idea there was another copy in that old Bible!"

"Shelby." Her mother's voice wasn't loud, but it was a command. "Ladies do not carry on in public. Compose yourself."

Shelby stopped sobbing, although she hiccupped several times. Dolly handed her a tissue box, and Shelby sat up straight, using several tissues to mop her face and blow her nose. "Mama," she said. "I'm so sorry. I've felt guilty about destroying those papers for a long time, but I didn't know what to do. I didn't think it would matter at that point in your life, when you'd been a Chisholm most of it and a Butler even longer."

"I accept your apology." Miss Cora's voice carried a thread of steel. "It's water under the bridge now, and we can't go back and change it." Her tone promised that they were not done with the discussion but that it would be conducted in private. She turned her attention back to Meredith and Julia. "As I said, I would like to meet my brother. And my sister as well."

Julia cleared her throat. "He, ah, he has not expressed any further wish to meet you, ma'am." Meredith was looking askance at her, but Julia figured Sumner deserved to have his say, and he wasn't here to do it himself. "I believe his feelings were terribly bruised by the rejection. He's a decorated veteran of World War II, and he was quite offended to have his honor impugned."

"I understand that," Miss Cora said. "Do you think if I wrote to him, that you could see it gets to him? Perhaps a letter of apology and explanation would heal the wound."

"It's certainly worth a try," Julia said.

"We'd be happy to deliver it," Meredith added.

"If you can return at one o'clock, I will have a letter prepared," Miss Cora said.

"There's something else," Julia said. She took a deep breath. "We used a contact at the *Savannah Morning News* to help us find your brother. She's the one who published the copy of the picture, although we did not authorize it. She asked me to let her know if my search yielded any results." She winced. "I didn't make her any promises, but I'm sure she hasn't forgotten that she asked."

Miss Cora looked down at her hands. "She should be rewarded for her assistance. If you hadn't found him, I'd never have known any of this, correct?"

Julia nodded.

"However," Miss Cora said, "I'm not keen on having my family's business splashed all over the paper for no reason. Let's wait and see if Sumner is willing to meet with me. If we reestablish some sort of relationship, I'd be amenable to having your reporter do a wrap-up type of story about how we were reunited. If not, then we'll just let it pass."

"That sounds fair to me," Julia said.

Meredith and Julia rose, and then Julia remembered something. She opened her purse and withdrew a sheaf of papers. "This is an interview Sumner's great-grandson did for a school project. It tells a little more about his life and his search for his siblings. You should have it."

One o'clock was only ninety minutes away. Just enough time to check in with Carmen at the agency and grab some lunch before making yet another—and hopefully, their final—trip to Guyton.

As Susan saw them out, and they started the short walk back to Magnolia Investigations, Meredith said, "We'd better not call, or he might refuse to see us."

"Exactly what I was thinking," Julia responded.

"Goodness, my mother would have a fit," Meredith said. "This makes twice in a week's time I've barged in on someone without calling."

That got a laugh out of Julia, although she wasn't feeling very amused at the moment. "Sometimes these situations call for an element of surprise."

Meredith snorted. "We still might not get through the door."

"We may not," Julia agreed soberly, thinking of Sumner Denton's stoic face.

***

They had lunch at Zunzi's after explaining to Carmen what had transpired during the meeting and what they'd be doing after they ate. Meredith ordered a Rising Sun, a vegan sandwich on French bread with portobello mushrooms, various vegetables and greens, avocado and hummus, and Zunzi's special sauces, while Julia had the Godfather, consisting of several meats, provolone and more, also on French bread. It had warmed up a bit, and they chose to sit outside at one of the tables beneath brightly colored umbrellas in the sun while a pair of tourists played cornhole at the boards set out front.

After the meal, they stopped by Miss Cora's, where Susan handed them the envelope. "Good luck," she told them. "I sure do hope he'll agree to meet with her." And then they began the drive out to Guyton again.

As they took the long driveway through the horse paddocks back to the sprawling ranch home, Julia felt the tension rise. "Are you as nervous as I am?" she asked Meredith.

"At least," Meredith said. "What are we going to do if he won't speak to her?"

"Make Shelby come out here and apologize in person," Julia said grimly. Then she relented. "I'm kidding. I think."

***

Sumner's grandson Leo, the father of the engaging Mason, answered the door this time. His features were as handsome as they had been the first time, but the look of welcoming inquiry faded into a stern frown as he realized who was standing on his front porch. "I'm afraid my grandfather isn't receiving callers this afternoon," he said, beginning to close the door.

"Oh, please wait," Meredith blurted.

Good manners made him hesitate, and Julia immediately said, "We're not here to harass your grandfather. We have a letter from his sister."

"If he doesn't want to read it, that's his choice," Meredith added, "but you should know she had nothing to do with turning him away three decades ago. Her daughter did it without her knowledge. Cora—Corie—would really like to meet Sumner."

Julia extended the letter. "We can wait in the car in case he has any questions."

Leo rolled his eyes and heaved a sigh. "My granddaddy would skin me alive if I made ladies wait outside. Come on in. I'll give him the letter. But if it upsets him too much, you'll have to go."

"Thank you," both women said at the same time, meekly following Leo into the house.

Chapter Eighteen

It was almost one o'clock on December twenty-third. Christmas was practically upon them, but this afternoon, Magnolia Investigations would be hosting a reunion. In just a few minutes, Cora Butler Chisholm, formerly Corie Denton, her biological brother, Sumner Denton, and her biological sister, Bobbie Dee Warrick, would all be arriving at the agency so Cora could meet her siblings for the first time in eighty-five years.

"Everything's ready." Carmen shot into the conference room, rearranging a pillow here, straightening the edge of a rug there. "I'll bring in refreshments as soon as everyone arrives and is settled."

Julia pressed a hand to her stomach. "I'm nervous. Big butterflies in here."

"Me too." Meredith blew out a breath. "I sure hope this goes well. Do you think Sumner will be hostile?"

"Or Bobbie Dee? We haven't even met her yet," Julia said. "I think it could go either way."

The bell over the front door jangled. "Showtime," Meredith murmured. "Smile, ladies."

Carmen hung back, letting Meredith and Julia greet the guests before they introduced her. Miss Cora was the first to arrive. She was accompanied only by her housekeeper and friend Susan. Julia was slightly relieved that Sumner wouldn't have to see his niece Shelby at this very first meeting, and she suspected Miss Cora had orchestrated that.

Meredith accompanied the two women to the conference room, and they were barely out of the foyer when the others arrived. Sumner and Bobbie Dee came in together, with Bobbie Dee's husband, Austin, Sumner's grandson Leo, and his great-grandson Mason following behind. The Warricks were staying with the Dentons for several days, and Leo had driven them all together in one vehicle. Julia led them to the conference room and stepped in ahead of Sumner.

There was a tense moment when Sumner entered the room and saw Miss Cora.

Miss Cora turned to face him. "Hello. I'm your sister Cora—whom you remember as Corie."

"It's nice to finally meet you," Sumner said.

Cora turned to Bobbie Dee. They looked so much alike, Julia realized. It was obvious there was a blood relationship. "And you're my big sister."

Bobbie Dee smiled tentatively. "My little sister Corie. You had these soft gold curls that I used to pull straight out just to see them spring back." She gestured to Miss Cora. "All over your head, those curls were."

"We have a lot to talk about," Miss Cora said. "A lot of good, and I guess some bad."

"We do," Sumner acknowledged.

Miss Cora tottered forward. "May I give you a hug?" Her voice quivered with suppressed emotion.

Sumner reached out, and Bobbie Dee stepped forward to join them. Three white heads bent together, reunited after so many years apart.

Bobbie Dee's husband, Austin, was wiping his eyes with a giant white handkerchief, while Leo blinked furiously. Mason, too young to be emotional, was beaming. Carmen offered Meredith and Susan tissues from a handily placed box and took one for herself. Julia looked away quickly, afraid she might sob as she felt Meredith reach for her hand.

Her gaze landed on the photocopy of the photograph of the five children, offered for sale over eight decades ago. It lay on a piecrust table in front of the window, where a crèche was arranged showing the Christ Child's birth in the humble manger.

"I must admit," Julia murmured to Meredith, "I wasn't sure for a while that we were going to be able to find the link between that photo and Miss Cora."

"And then I wasn't sure we were going to get that happy ending that we wanted," Meredith added.

"Shelby really is sorry," Julia said. "Miss Cora said she badly wanted to come today, but agreed that an in-person apology could wait until after the initial reunion was over."

"I think this is perfect," Meredith said as Carmen slipped out the door to fetch the light refreshments they had planned. "A Christmas reunion."

"It's the season of miracles," Julia said. "How lovely that we were able to be a part of making this one happen."

Dear Reader,

When my son-in-law, a Blackhawk pilot, was posted to Hunter Army Airfield in midtown Savannah in 2012, our family was excited. We'd have a great vacation destination! Little did I realize that only four short years later, I'd be packing up my Pennsylvania home for a move to "the Hostess City of the South."

Life in Savannah was completely different from anything I'd ever known. The climate, steaming in summer and pleasant in winter, was an adjustment. Landscaping and planting, one of my particular joys, was quite foreign in the new climate. The bugs, over-sized and everywhere, were another adjustment. Still, largely thanks to my animal rescue and wildlife rehab volunteerism, I made many wonderful friends who introduced me to life in "The Sav." My husband worked downtown in the Historic District, and my grand-daughter went to preschool at Wesley Monumental. I routinely walked in Forsyth Park or around Lake Mayer each morning. We ate at dozens of restaurants, some famous, some known more to local folks, and enjoyed the beaches of Tybee Island frequently.

Two years later, my husband's job took us "home" to State College, Pennsylvania, again. Returning to a familiar location, to a familiar climate and back to so many friends and family felt like slip-ping back into a comfortable set of clothes. But I treasure the memo-ries and friendships from my Savannah years. Writing this book immersed me in so many "feel-good" memories, and I hope you'll enjoy reading about Savannah from an insider's point of view.

Wishing you many holiday blessings,
Anne Marie

About the Author

ANNE MARIE RODGERS HAS WRITTEN over twenty inspirational and inspirational mystery novels for Guideposts Books and almost five dozen books in her publishing career, including a number of best-sellers and award winners. Anne Marie is deeply committed to giving a voice to the world's animals who cannot speak for themselves. She has worked in emergency veterinary care and volunteered in wildlife rehabilitation, canine training and foster care, service dog puppy raising, and neonatal orphaned kitten rescue, which includes bottle feeding over four hundred kittens. She currently works for a day veterinary practice. Anne Marie and her husband delight in their family, which includes four grandchildren and a varying number of furry family members. In 2019, they adopted a blind, diabetic Labrador retriever who refuses to believe he is handicapped.

The Truth Behind the Fiction

I HAD NO IDEA WHAT type of historical mystery I might explore, even a few weeks before it was time to begin work on this novel. And then I happened across an historic photograph originally published in the *Vidette-Messenger* of Valparaiso, Indiana, on August 5, 1948. The photo shows a woman standing on a porch, hiding her face in an apron, while four children sit on porch steps before her, next to a sign reading: "4 Children for Sale. Inquire within."

In the accompanying story, I learned that all four children, and a fifth yet to be born, were indeed sold or adopted in 1948. The surviving children eventually found each other and compared their life stories, which were not for the faint of heart. What if, I thought, my mystery involved the ladies of Magnolia Investigations reuniting long-separated siblings who had been torn apart in a similar type of situation? However, because this is fiction and I have a soft heart, in my novel, I gave most of the siblings happier endings than the poor little souls in that photograph received.

MACARONS
(MAKES 30)

INGREDIENTS:

Note: You will need a food processor, icing piping bag with round tip, and parchment paper.

Almond Macaron Shells:

1¾ cups powdered sugar

1 cup almond flour, finely ground

1 teaspoon salt, divided

3 egg whites, at room temperature

¼ cup granulated sugar

½ teaspoon vanilla extract

2 drops pink gel food coloring

Vanilla Buttercream Filling:

1 cup unsalted butter, 2 sticks, at room temperature

3 cups powdered sugar

1 teaspoon vanilla extract

3 tablespoons heavy cream

DIRECTIONS:

Macaron Shells:

In the bowl of food processor, combine powdered sugar, almond flour, and ½ teaspoon of salt. Process on low speed until extra fine. Sift almond flour mixture through fine-mesh sieve into large bowl.

In separate large bowl, beat egg whites and remaining ½ teaspoon of salt with electric hand mixer until soft peaks form. Gradually add granulated sugar until fully incorporated. Continue to beat until stiff peaks form and nothing moves if you turn the bowl upside down. Add vanilla and beat until incorporated. Add food coloring and beat until just combined. Add about ⅓ sifted almond flour mixture at a time to the beaten egg whites, using spatula to gently fold until combined. After last addition of almond flour, continue to fold slowly until batter falls into ribbons and you can make a figure eight while holding spatula up.

Transfer macaron batter into piping bag fitted with round tip. Place 4 dots of batter in each corner of rimmed baking sheet. Place 1 sheet parchment paper over it, using batter to help adhere parchment to baking sheet.

Pipe macarons onto parchment paper in 1½-inch (3-cm) circles, spacing at least 1 inch apart. Tap baking sheet on flat surface 5 times to release air bubbles.

Let set at room temperature for 30 minutes to 1 hour until dry to the touch.

Preheat oven to 300°F (150°C). Bake for 17 minutes until they are well risen and don't stick to parchment paper. Transfer the macarons to wire rack; must cool completely before filling.

Buttercream Filling:

In large bowl, add butter and beat with mixer for 1 minute until light and fluffy. Sift in powdered sugar and beat until fully incorporated. Add vanilla and beat to combine. Add cream, 1 tablespoon at a time, and beat to combine, until desired consistency is reached.

Transfer buttercream to piping bag fitted with round tip.

Add 1 dollop of buttercream to 1 macaron shell. Top with second macaron shell to create "sandwich." Repeat with remaining macaron shells and buttercream.

Serving Instructions:

Place completed macarons in airtight container for 24 hours before serving and eating.

Read on for a sneak peek of another exciting book
in the Savannah Secrets series!

Southern Fried Secrets

BY NANCY MEHL

MEREDITH BELLEFONTAINE FROWNED AS SHE watched her partner in Magnolia Investigations stare at a file on her lap. Julia had been in her office all morning, going through their files, trying to whittle down any unnecessary paperwork. It was clear her heart wasn't really in it. She sat in one of the two chairs in front of Meredith's desk, using the other chair to stack the files she'd cleaned out.

Outside, the rain tapped on the roof and drizzled down the large floor-to-ceiling windows in Meredith's office. Usually she loved rainy days, but for some reason, today it just added to the feeling of boredom she felt. She liked to keep the temperature in her office a little chilly, but in deference to Julia she'd started a small fire in the fireplace. It crackled and popped, adding to the cozy ambience of the room.

"Carmen can take care of that," Meredith said, pointing at the files. "It's actually her job, you know."

"I realize that, but she's not here and I need something to do."

Carmen Lopez, their receptionist, had been out for over a week with the flu. Chatty, funny, and extremely competent, she added a sense of fun to every day. She was certainly missed.

"We need a case," Meredith said, stating the obvious.

Julia sighed. "No kidding. If I keep cleaning out these files, the only thing left will be the folder itself."

Meredith laughed and looked at her watch. "It's almost eleven. Maybe we should take an early lunch and…"

The front door opened, and a few seconds later a tall man stepped into Meredith's office. She was surprised to see he didn't have an umbrella. Water dripped off his longish gray hair and beard. When his eyes met hers, Meredith realized she knew him. "Davis," she said with a smile. "How nice to see you."

"You're Davis Hedgerow," Julia said. "You write that wonderful column in the *Savannah Tribune*, 'Searching Savannah.'" She stood up and shook his hand. "I never miss it."

Davis wrote about well-known Savannah attractions as well as places even older residents didn't know about. "I haven't seen you since the funeral," Meredith said.

"I know," Davis said. "Sorry. I've wanted to stop by and check on you. Maybe you could come over one day soon. You know how much Sally loves to cook."

He grinned at her, and Meredith giggled. "Sally is very brave in the kitchen," she said to Julia. "Let's just say that some of her more complicated recipes aren't always successful."

"In other words, they're awful," Davis said. "Like the vegetarian gumbo with tofu. She proved that gumbo with tofu isn't gumbo at all. I still can't believe you and Ron ate an entire bowl. I wasn't brave enough to make it across the finish line."

Davis and Julia laughed, but then Meredith watched as his expression changed. "Have a seat," she said, gesturing to one of the chairs in front of her desk. Julia picked up the files she'd put on the seat and carefully placed them on the floor next to her.

"I'm here," he said as he sat down, "because I…might need some help."

"Might?" Meredith asked.

Davis reached into the pocket of his lightweight overcoat and pulled out a blue envelope. "This was given to the receptionist at the paper last week. And before you ask, no, she doesn't remember anything about the person who gave it to her. All kinds of packages and mail are delivered to her throughout the day, and she also answers tons of phone calls. Eventually the letter was sent upstairs to me. And there's something strange about the way the letter was dropped off at the newspaper's desk. I've seen the security footage. The guy who brought it was careful not to draw attention to himself. Wore a hat and kept his face hidden from the security cameras. That makes me think he scouted things out before delivering the letter." He handed the envelope to Meredith, who opened it slowly.

"So this went through quite a few people before you got it?" Meredith asked.

"I suppose. The receptionist. The mail room where the mail is sorted. The guy who delivers the mail… I would say it traveled quite a bit before I got it." He frowned at her. "Why?"

"Fingerprints," Julia said. "Now add Meredith and you to the list." She shrugged. "Too many people have touched it. I doubt seriously we can get anything from it."

"I don't think you'll find any fingerprints from the person who delivered the letter. The video showed that he wore gloves."

"If he was trying to keep his fingerprints off the envelope I'm pretty sure he didn't leave any on the letter either." Meredith carefully removed the folded piece of paper, using a tissue to hold it. She opened it and began to read. PUBLISH YOUR NEW BOOK AT YOUR OWN PERIL. IF YOU DON'T STOP ITS PUBLICATION YOU'LL BE SORRY. VERY SORRY. Block letters. Plain white paper. Nothing distinctive about it. She handed it to Julia, along with the tissue. "No signature of course."

"Do you have any idea who wrote this?" Julia asked after reading it. She gave it back to Meredith.

Davis shook his head. "Not a clue. I mean, my upcoming book is mostly a compilation of my past articles about Savannah attractions. Not some kind of exposé that would compromise anyone."

"Maybe he has a similar book coming out?" Julia suggested. "Could this person be afraid your book will steal sales from him?"

"The same thought occurred to me, so I did a little poking around. Couldn't find anything like that. Besides, I think most people in Savannah look to me for this kind of information. I really can't see a legitimate publisher signing someone to compete with me. I don't mean that to sound egotistical. I'm just stating facts."

"I understand," Meredith said. "This could be a prank, you know. It may mean nothing."

"I realize that, but even before the letter arrived I had a weird feeling. Like I was being watched."

"Watched?" Julia echoed. "What do you mean? You think this guy followed you to the newspaper?"

"No, not necessarily." Davis rubbed the back of his neck. He was clearly under stress. "The other night when I got home, I was convinced someone was hiding in the bushes that run along my property line. I went outside to check it out, but no one was there. I talked myself into believing it was the neighbor's cat. But then it happened again the very next night." His eyes sought Meredith's. "Sally is alone a lot because of my work. She gets out some, but all in all, she's a real homebody. I'm...I'm not sure she's safe."

Meredith put the letter back in the envelope and handed it to Davis. "You need the police, Davis. Not us. We're investigators, not bodyguards."

"I realize that. But what if this really is some kind of a prank and word gets out? I'm in the public eye. And besides... Well, I'm afraid my publisher might get cold feet if I come off like some kind of nut afraid of his own shadow. Or even that I'm lying in an attempt to draw attention to my book."

"But wouldn't attention to your book be a good thing?" Julia asked.

"Not if the publisher thinks I made it up. Makes me look unprofessional." He sighed deeply. "I know I sound paranoid, but this same publisher recently had an author who faked cancer because she thought more people would purchase her book. When the truth came out, they took a big hit. I don't want this to remind them of that fiasco."

Davis slumped down in the chair. "This book is really important to me. And not just because of the money I hope it'll make. I've given my publisher a proposal for a line of books, each one highlighting attractions in other cities. Sally and I would get to travel together on their dime. She's had a tough time lately. Her mother passed away suddenly. They were very close. I think getting away from Savannah and visiting other places would really help her. I just can't allow anything to ruin this deal." He put the envelope on Meredith's desk. "I'm convinced that this effort to stop publication is connected to one of the five new businesses mentioned in the book."

Meredith wasn't convinced Davis was on the right path. "Look, Davis, I'm just not sure about this. Did you write something negative about any of these new places?"

"No. I only highlight attractions I believe people will enjoy. If I investigate it and feel it's not exceptional, I don't write about it."

"I'm confused," Julia said. "How would anyone know what's in a book that isn't available yet?"

"The publisher has sent out quite a few ARCs—Advanced Readers Copies. They go to TV stations, other publishers and media outlets, and, of course, to anyone associated with the sites in the book. A few copies were mailed to city hall so they could mention the book and the new attractions on Savannah's official website."

"Could this be someone you decided not to include in the book?" Meredith asked, trying to come up with any reasonable possibilities.

"I thought about that, but there's no one. Every one of the new sites was recommended by a friend or reader who had either visited the place or who had heard about it from someone else. No one was rejected."

"What about a past business that didn't like what you wrote?" Meredith asked.

"No. There's no one like that. For the other locations I just gave my editor the original article I wrote on each one, and she added them without any changes. If any of those sites were upset about what I wrote, they would have said something long ago, when their article first came out. All of them were thrilled for a mention." He clasped his hands together. "Look, I know in my gut someone connected with one of these five new places is behind this letter."

Although he didn't look angry, Davis was firm. Meredith could see he wasn't going to budge. She wanted to help her old friend, but was this a case they should take? Were the parameters Davis had given them too narrow? Would it end up being a wild goose chase or were his instincts right? Meredith looked at Julia. Her expression echoed Meredith's hesitation. What were they getting into?

A Note from the Editors

WE HOPE YOU ENJOY THE Savannah Secrets series, created by the Books and Inspirational Media Division of Guideposts, a nonprofit organization that touches millions of lives every day through products and services that inspire, encourage, help you grow in your faith, and celebrate God's love in every aspect of your daily life.

Thank you for making a difference with your purchase of this book, which helps fund our many outreach programs to military personnel, prisons, hospitals, nursing homes, and educational institutions. To learn more, visit GuidepostsFoundation.org.

We also maintain many useful and uplifting online resources. Visit Guideposts.org to read true stories of hope and inspiration, access OurPrayer network, sign up for free newsletters, download free e-books, join our Facebook community, and follow our stimulating blogs.

To learn about other Guideposts publications, including the bestselling devotional *Daily Guideposts*, go to ShopGuideposts.org, call (800) 932-2145, or write to Guideposts, PO Box 5815, Harlan, Iowa 51593.

Sign up for the Guideposts Fiction Newsletter

and stay up-to-date on the books you love!

You'll get sneak peeks of new releases, recommendations from other Guideposts readers, and special offers just for you . . .

and it's FREE!

Just go to Guideposts.org/Newsletters today to sign up.

Guideposts.

Visit Guideposts.org/Shop
or call (800) 932-2145